GUNSMOKE AND HEXES

TALES FROM THE CURSED FRONTIER

ROSS CARMONA, OSCAR CHAVIRA, JR., GEORGE COTTONWOOD, TONY GARCIA, CURTIS MOORE, MICHAEL JOHN PETTY, & BENJAMIN WINTERS

EDGE WEAVER LLC

Gunsmoke and Hexes
Tales from the Cursed Frontier

Edge Weaver Realms is an imprint of Edge Weaver LLC

Copyright © 2025, Edge Weaver

Stories curated by Marie Ito.

Edited by Bryn Reed and Marie Ito

Cover by: CBScout

Book Design: Marie Ito

Kindle ISBN: 978-1-968100-18-6

Paperback ISBN: 978-1-968100-19-3

Published in the United States of America

Edge Weaver LLC
19360 Rinaldi #681
Porter Ranch, CA 91326-1607

CONTENTS

FLESH AND BLOOD

BY: BENJAMIN WINTERS

The sun was setting on the West and God had left His grave. On the rapidly cooling Easter evening of April 21st, 1889, Daniel Carol lay in a ditch near his father, Robert. The naturally formed ditch once linked back to the Canadian River, the southern boundary of the newly opening Oklahoma Country, but was now a mostly dry channel keeping the Carols out of sight. Robert had expected to cross the Canadian before nightfall, but the trees were sparse, and U.S. Troops were patrolling for any early entry of the Unassigned Lands. Robert didn't like the idea of crossing the river in the dark, especially after the recent rains had caused the river to rise and flood in some stretches, and he liked even less having Daniel with him. Robert had three sons: two of them were capable, and Daniel was the third. Robert didn't understand why Daniel was so different from his brothers or why he stirred Robert's temper so easily, but it made Robert uncomfortable and, therefore, made Daniel a burden to be around. A night-crossing of an angry river wasn't a good idea, but waiting until noon tomorrow to cross with the caravan was unacceptable. Robert was determined to get to the North Canadian River just before noon tomorrow, come Hell or high water.

Daniel was surprised when his father directed him to walk with him. Daniel did not particularly enjoy his father's company, and his father made it no secret that the feeling was mutual. The previous evening, Daniel's father made a show of taking Daniel with him through the Caravan camp, rifles in hand, telling people they were going to work on Daniel's aim by shooting what they could scare up. This embarrassed Daniel greatly, but he didn't dare contradict his father in front of the others. They made their way out past the white sails of the wagons and through the horses, who were busy grazing on any grass they could reach while tied up, and kept going until Daniel could no longer hear individual shouts or calls but just a low constant thrum of a thousand voices whispering in the prairie winds.

Between the gusts of wind, Daniel blurted, "My aim is fine, I don't need to practice."

Robert stopped, barely raised the barrel of his repeater above his knee, and fired a round into the dirt. Daniel began to open his mouth to ask what his father was doing before Robert looked him in the eye and cut him off.

"We ain't out here for practice. We're out here to make a racket until sunset, so our neighbors don't question why we left the camp. We will start walking north into the Unassigned Lands once it gets dark enough," Robert said.

"But nobody is supposed to go in there until Monday; we'll get stopped by the army!" Daniel said.

"No," Robert said, shaking his head with something approximating a sneer towards the ground between them. "We're gonna be quiet and move in the dark so that the troops don't spot us. I guarantee there are already dozens, if not hundreds, of folks who have passed the barrier. If we don't go in early, we won't get a scrap of land, and this entire venture will be worthless."

"You and I don't have any food or water or horses to make that long of a journey," Daniel said.

"I've already considered that!" Robert felt his irritation boil over into indignation with Daniel. The boy wasn't wrong for asking about the supplies or the plan; indeed, it demonstrated some basic intelligence. Robert couldn't place his finger on why, but he felt that someone as uninvolved and inept as Daniel usually was shouldn't demand answers and should instead just do as he's told. Just follow orders, like a soldier, even when it doesn't make sense, even if hurts, like Robert did when he was around Daniel's age. Robert cleared his mind, racked another round in the chamber, and fired off a second shot, continuing, "Billy dropped off our supplies outside of camp this morning when he took his horse out for water. You and I won't be taking none of the horses. We will have to walk the whole way, which is why we are leaving tonight. Your mother and brothers will follow up with the rest of the caravan on Monday."

"Why me? Why not Billy or Sammy? Billy is old enough to make a claim for land, too, and Sammy can't stand waiting on all the slow wagons," Daniel said.

"Sammy can fix the wagon should anything break, and Billy can keep the horses calm crossing the river, and your mother talks too much, so people would notice if she is gone. But you just sit with your nose in a book all day, ain't nobody gonna notice your absence. Once we get to our destination, you are going to do what you do best: sit. And hopefully, by sitting on our land, you will deter any late arrivals from stealing it, while I make our claim with the Land Office. If I could make it work any other way and leave you with your mother, I would," Robert said.

Daniel gritted his teeth and stared straight into his father's eyes. He was no stranger to his father's cruel remarks, but he had fooled himself into thinking that his father might have chosen him for a good reason and felt shamefully stupid for that. He could feel moisture building on the edges of his eyes, and before he could shame himself further, he turned, raised his rifle, and fired at the shrinking sun.

Twilight turned to dusk with Daniel and Robert standing apart in a silence only occasionally interrupted by gunfire. Robert eventually turned north and began walking. Daniel followed after his father, the time in silence failing to cool his anger or lessen his humiliation. Thinking about his father's remarks made his blood boil, but he couldn't put his mind to any other task. As soon as he forced his thoughts on to some other topic, his mind would wind back to the conversation and make him fume.

Daniel didn't sit reading all the time. He worked just as much as his older brothers, he just got the mindless tasks and they got the interesting ones. Billy loved the horses, so he didn't mind working with them and trimming their hooves or brushing them. Sammy liked to whittle and especially liked to do so away from the house so that no one would remember to give him extra work.

Sammy had to learn how to keep blades sharp, and the tools well oiled, and the wood shavings he made only happened to be useful for fire. Daniel did his chores, but in his little free time, he liked to read. Sometimes, he would read a little between chores, and sometimes, while carrying a sack of grain on his shoulder or hauling a bucket of water to the house, he would use his free hand to hold up a book to read while he worked. Unlike his brothers' hobbies, reading didn't provide any secondary benefits to the household. It also didn't help that his father always appeared when Daniel was reading and assumed Daniel never set his books down. His brothers knew him and his work better, but they weren't in the business of correcting their father. That was a theme all of Daniel's childhood: his brothers looking the other way when their father found cause to express his displeasure.

As the night grew deeper, the wind became sharp with cold, cutting through Daniel's clothes and turning his evening's sweat into bitter patches of chill. The cold cooled Daniel's temper as effectively as it cooled his body. If Daniel was honest with himself, he did deserve his father's wrath at times. He knew he could be difficult to work with. His father would ask him to do a chore, and instead of jumping to the task, he would try to hand it off to one of his brothers. Even his mother was moved to whip him with whatever was available in the house when he forgot a chore or complained about working. If he could make his mother, the nicest person he knew, that angry, then surely something must be wrong with him. He must have earned the rod at least some of the time. As Daniel walked, he felt guilty, guilty for being the wrong kind of person, guilty for being a bad son. Maybe with this new land, he could be a new person, a beloved son, maybe even a son his father liked.

Robert made it to the supplies and was glad that Mary had packed everything so efficiently. It made it easier for Billy to sneak out on his horse, but she also anticipated what they would need first and organized the items within to be accessible. Robert untied the leather cords that held the jackets around the buffalo hide blanket. Robert handed Daniel his coat first and then put his own on. Water canteens that were insulated and held down by the coats were now uncovered and ready for use. Robert handed one to Daniel, who eagerly drank from his, and slung the other over his shoulder. The last item sitting on the buffalo hide was some bacon wrapped in cheese-cloth. Robert split the bacon and then picked up the buffalo skin bundle, which contained the rest of the tools they would need.

Robert walked northwest, keeping an ear out for the sound of the Canadian River ahead. They would follow the river northeast for nearly twenty miles, then cut straight north for another ten past the river. Nearly thirty miles of wilderness, on foot, mainly in the dark, and with only forty hours until everyone with a horse comes chasing after. "God Almighty," Robert thought, "we should have left yesterday."

The duo, with a little bacon in them and wrapped in warm coats, moved with a new vigor. Robert was initially absorbed in the work of collecting the supplies, checking for any onlookers or patrols, and finding safe footing in the dark. Tasks he hadn't done since the war but that came back to him as easy as riding a horse. There was comfort in focusing on the work, but as time progressed, he found his mind returning to the conversation earlier this evening. He knew he was too harsh with Daniel, or he was likely just too harsh in general. But then again, maybe he wasn't stern enough. Perhaps he had never been stern enough, and now Daniel was ruined goods because of it. Robert didn't remember raising Daniel any differently than Billy or Sammy, and those boys were far from perfect, but Robert understood them and knew how to get his message across to them. With Daniel, it was different.

The boy just didn't share the same values or appreciate the right things. Robert remembered smiling when he saw Daniel first reading, especially after he and Mary had to tie Sammy to a chair and force him to learn his letters. His pride in Daniel's easy reading gave way to frustration from all the things Daniel couldn't or wouldn't do. He was an embarrassment with a lariat, a liability with an axe, and messy with a shovel. Robert recalled teaching Billy different kinds of knots and how they should be used, and he remembered how Billy shared what he learned with Sammy. He also remembered how much Sammy loved listening to him explain the proper way to skin a deer and even asked to do it the next time they brought one down. Robert could not recall Daniel ever being that attentive or enthusiastic about a lesson . . . though, as he plodded through the moonlight, it began to trouble Robert that he was struggling to think of any specific lessons he had taught to Daniel directly.

Daniel now realized why his father had insisted that he and his brothers walk with the caravan instead of riding in the wagon or with one of the horses. Daniel assumed his father just got tired of seeing him reading, so to spite him, Daniel had read his book while walking behind the wagon. Now Daniel understood that his father had been preparing him for the grueling journey they now faced. He wondered if his brothers also had to walk with him behind the wagon to avoid sus-picion from their fellow travelers or if his father hadn't yet known who would accompany him into Oklahoma Country. Daniel wished he could read now, but there was little light and it wouldn't be safe to walk in the dark without paying attention. Daniel had a small dime novel in his back pocket about some outlaws who stole from the rich and gave to the poor. He had traded for the book with another book of his own to a young member of the caravan. In fact, Daniel had traded books with other travelers the entire way up from Texas and one time accidentally traded for a book he had already read. It was a good one though, so he didn't mind. Daniel wanted this journey to be like the stories he read, filled with adventure and with him playing the hero, but this entire trip, just like tonight, was just a long tiring walk with no way to know what lay ahead.

Robert halted and Daniel had to balance on his toes to keep from falling forward. Daniel followed his father's sightline and spotted the dark silhouette of someone on horseback ahead of them. A slouched figure on a horse slowly made its way towards them, the moonlight glinting off the metal of the rider's rifle. Robert slowly crouched and Daniel followed suit. The rider crept towards them but spoke no words and did not alter his pace. The deep blue garb of the soldier looked black in the poor light, but the rifle slung over his lap gleamed like it was made from silver and copper. Daniel's heart was pounding so hard that he could feel the drumming in his throat and ears. He wanted to take off like a jackrabbit and find a hole to hide in. Another part of him also wanted to call out and put an end to this journey.

Robert's pulse was quickened by the sight of the man and only slightly slowed when he realized it was a soldier and not some outlaw or Comanche looking to fight. As the rider drew closer, Robert considered what he might do should the soldier perceive them. Was it better to be turned back and risk everything in the land rush or to end this rider's journey and risk the wrath of his comrades? Robert had heard that the troops were stretched thin and were mainly focused on shepherding the thousands of wagons on the main trails, but were they thinned out enough to miss one of their own? The rider was almost on top of them and Robert placed his thumb on the hammer of his repeater.

Daniel could feel his body shaking with fright, and he willed himself to be still so he wouldn't give himself away. The rider was nearly on top of them and Daniel couldn't believe the soldier hadn't hailed them. The rider's horse whinnied and Daniel felt faint from the sudden sound. The soldier sat up straight and pulled his horse to a halt.

"Whut iss it? We goh uh ssnaake in the grass, girrl?" the rider slurred to his horse.

The horse's right eye met Robert's gaze and the beast shook its head back and forth.

"Fine, less go thiss way then," the soldier ordered by pulling the reins to his left. The horse turned away from Robert and Daniel and dutifully carried her inebriated cargo away.

After the patrol got out of sight, Robert removed his thumb from the hammer and stood. He didn't like how close they had just come to conflict, but he took some solace in the fact his nerves hadn't gotten the better of him. He was taking his family north to escape the escalating hostilities of land disputes and to avoid being drawn into another armed conflict, but he was worried that he would be pressed into violence before all of this was over. Daniel, who moments before had wanted to sprint away, now felt utterly drained and wanted to just lie down and sleep, but his father returned to the trek and Daniel reluctantly followed.

Coyote yips and howls began to fill the air after midnight. The calls were chaotic and disorganized. Daniel couldn't imagine how many there must have been to create so many sounds at once. The sounds were close; maybe a quarter of a mile away, Daniel guessed. He gripped his rifle tighter and hoped the coyotes found different prey. Robert didn't usually care for the incessant racket the coyotes caused, but tonight, he was thankful for them. Their shrieking banter would provide excellent cover for him and Daniel to move unheard.

The coyotes kept up their song for several hours, but a mist sprawled over the prairie and enveloped Daniel and Robert. On the one hand, Robert was glad the mist was obscuring them further, making them invisible as well as silent. On the other hand, Robert didn't like the loss of visibility he suffered from the mist. He turned slightly to go directly north to intercept the river instead of walking parallel to it as he had planned. If he got close enough to hear the river, he could make his way alongside it without getting lost in the mist, but with the coyote chorus ongoing, Robert would have to get within a couple of hundred feet of the river to hear it.

The mist was refreshing to Daniel as it pulled him from his marching-induced stupor. The terror of the coyotes' proximity waned as they never sounded any closer and certainly had more than enough time to run Daniel and his father down. The mist made it hard to see his father right in front of him, but Daniel knew they were heading directly to the river, so he could catch up if they got separated for a moment.

Robert was wrong; the river was louder than he had anticipated. The river was flooding over in areas and reaching the lip of the shore elsewhere. The current was strong, and the noise of the water crashing against the trees and rocks made Robert forget all about the calls in the night. The river was alive and angry, and Robert grew worried about their eventual crossing. They wouldn't be able to find a narrow crossing point in all this mist, so they would have to keep walking until the mist cleared or the sun came out.

Daniel was standing in water but was still hundreds of feet from the river. It was unlikely that the river would be much better tomorrow, and he was not eager to attempt passing it. While he reflected on the danger they would face, his eyes were drawn to a faint green light that pierced the mist. The light looked to be several miles down the river but moving slowly up towards them. Daniel tapped his father's shoulder and gestured toward the odd green light.

Robert saw the light moving slowly up the river but he wasn't sure how. He shouldn't be able to see a light from that far away with all this mist. Robert even walked forward a distance and waved his hand to make sure he wasn't seeing some firefly. Once he determined that the light was indeed a great distance away and flowing up the river, he concluded that it had to be a boat—but who in their right mind would travel the river in this state? There was also something else about that creeping light that unsettled Robert deeply; it had an unnatural way about it.

Robert recalled a time in his youth when a rabid skunk crawled into the chicken shed. The creature's mouth was covered in foam and left a trail of slime and blood behind it. The animal didn't move in a straight line but lumbered at an angle like it was pulling itself forward with only one of its paws. It had a constant low growl that would hitch momentarily from effort as the skunk altered its direction. The hair of the skunk was disheveled and frayed in places, matted down, and clumped from drool in others. For a moment, Robert had thought the skunk was dead and something unseen must be dragging it forward. Robert's father shot the skunk and then they burned the body and turned over the earth where the skunk had crawled. Robert's mother had refused to collect the eggs from the chickens for a week. While disease was just as natural as breathing, something about that rabid animal was unnatural, evil. When Robert stared into the green light on the river, he saw that twisted creature's drooling mouth.

Robert's reflections came to a grinding halt when the sound of a hammer cocked behind him and Daniel.

"Don't get funny now. I don't mean to be impolite but people wandering in the dark might be dangerous, like myself. So soothe my fears and put your rifles on the ground real slow like," the stranger said.

Daniel looked to his father to see what he should do. They were at a disadvantage with their backs to the stranger and they didn't know if the man was alone, but Daniel knew his father was a trained soldier and Daniel figured the dark helped as much as it hurt. They might be able to shoot their way out of this.

Robert saw Daniel's look and shook his head. Their best chance was to follow the request of the stranger. The stranger wouldn't want to risk the noise of a gunfight if he didn't have to and the stranger's voice, while light-hearted, had a steel edge that Robert knew well. This man would pull the trigger if it came to it. Robert set his rifle down, wincing as the gun touched the standing water on the oversaturated ground. Daniel, thankfully, did likewise.

"Well buffalo in a biscuit, this isn't a land of only outlaws and drunkards as I had been led to believe. Now we can introduce ourselves like civilized folks. Since I'm aiming a pistol at you, I will go first. I'm Joe Hines, pistolero and De-Regulator," Joe said. "Now you two introduce yourselves.

"Daniel Carol, sir," Daniel said without thinking. He winced and looked to his father apologetically.

Robert clenched his jaw, released it, and simply said, "Robert."

"Pleasure to make your acquaintances on this suspicious night," Joe said.

"I think you mean auspicious," Daniel said, and then added, "I mean, that's what they say in the stories is all, Mr. Hines."

"Nope, I meant suspicious, and please call me Joe," Joe replied.

"Alright, what do you want from us Joe?" Robert asked.

Joe uncocked the hammer on his pistol and returned it to his holster. "I don't want nothing from you. I was merely surveying the area when you got too close for comfort and I thought I would rattle my tail so you wouldn't tread on me by mistake."

"Well, we can be on our way and let you slither back to your surveys," Robert stated.

"I have questions that I need you to answer before I get to my slithering," said Joe.

"Fine, let's hear them and be on our way," Robert said.

"Firstly, have either of you come across a rough looking crew selling spirits tonight?" Joe raised a finger at the first question and then raised another to count off the next one. "Secondly, can you find it in your heart to share some of the food you must be carrying? I'm famished."

The group moved to dry ground where Joe had left his horse tied up. Robert and Daniel were permitted to collect their rifles and now they all sat on the grass eating dry rations in the dark to avoid drawing any additional attention.

"I've been tracking this real nasty crew up from Texas. They used to run with the Regulators in New Mexico and then joined the Blue Devils in Texas to rough up farmers. Most recently, they murdered and robbed a man who was hauling liquor to these unassigned lands. He intended to open a saloon, but the bandits opened him up instead. I think they bribed one of the patrols with liquor to let them cross the river early, but I don't know where precisely they crossed," Joe told them.

"We passed by a patrol, and he seemed well into the drink," Daniel said.

"We passed him not long before you found us. I would guess your bandits crossed further northwest," Robert offered.

"I'm getting closer, and their time is running out," Joe said.

"You seem awfully confident for a single man who is planning to face a whole crew of armed men," Robert said.

"We've crossed paths before. When they see me again, they'll be seeing a ghost and they will be terrified. Plus, they will probably be drunk, so I like my odds. That said, I won't turn down extra guns if you two want to help me mete out justice. I would split the bounties with you," Joe explained.

"We don't have the time or inclination to join a shootout. We're just trying to secure some farmland, not die for someone else's liquor," Robert said.

Joe didn't respond but instead stared out at the green light on the river. Even though they had moved back from the river, the light had grown in intensity and appeared much closer than before.

"Do you know what that light is, Mr. Hines?" Daniel asked.

"I've heard the stories, and I confess, I believe them," Joe said.

"What have you heard?" Daniel said.

"The stories say that light is the ghostly glow of the *J.R. Williams*, a Union steamboat that was sunk by General Stand Watie and his Confederate soldiers. The ship was carrying food and didn't have enough men to protect it. The Confederates ambushed the boat from the shore, boarded it, killed part of the crew, took what they could carry of the supplies, and then set it on fire so that the Union couldn't recover anything. The boat went to the bottom of the river where the Canadian and the Arkansas meet, which is why people claim to see it all over the territories. An old Shawnee woman told me that the slaughtered crew members kidnap children from their beds for stealing and take them to the coyotes." Joe paused to listen to the coyotes' song. "She also said the Coyote went bad and isn't a friend to mankind anymore. I didn't know what she meant but all the campfire stories tell it the same. The coyotes call, the river water rises, and with it the green glowing corpse of the *J.R. Williams*."

"That's a wheelbarrow full of manure," Robert said.

But the story rattled him. Not because of the story itself but because Robert recalled a different ship taken by the Confederates, the *USS Harriet Lane*, at the Battle of Galveston. Robert remembered the chaos and confusion of the battle. The cheers when he and his crewmates sank the *CS Neptune*, then fear when the enemy fired on the *Harriet Lane* and crippled it, and finally the betrayal when friendly fire struck the ship to destroy it and deny the use of it to the enemy. Somehow the *USS Harriet Lane* stayed afloat, undead, ready to be enthralled by the Confederacy. It all ended when the *CS Bayou City* rammed the starboard side of the ship and flooded the deck with soldiers. Like the coyotes and the *J.R. Williams*, the Confederacy resurrected the *Harriet Lane* and put it to work dragging young men to their deaths. Robert recalled diving overboard into the churning sea to escape. He remembered grabbing a hand that didn't return his grasp, one of the bodies of his fallen comrades, which tossed in the waves, clashing into other bodies and the *Harriet Lane*, at the mercy of the currents. Robert dove deeper to get clear of the obstacles and conflict and in the dark water below Robert saw something, something he convinced himself was just a case of Soldier's Heart, a fever dream from the heat of battle: two bright green eyes and a jagged maw wreathed in foam and blood looking up at him. Smiling.

Robert was saved from his reverie by Daniel. "Couldn't it be true? Doesn't Matthew's Gospel say the dead rose on Good Friday? That was yesterday and tomorrow is Easter, when the Lord raised from the grave too. Could resurrection be possible every Easter?"

"Let's hope not, as that could make my hunt tricky to complete," Joe said.

"I won't have us mixing lies with the Good Book. Mr. Hines, if that's your real name, I wouldn't worry if I was you, only good people will see the resurrection. Neither you nor your quarry have to worry about that," Robert said.

"Well, thank God for that I suppose," Joe said, smirking in spite of the implication.

"We've wasted enough time with stories. Daniel, we need to get back to it," Robert said. He stood, grabbed his rifle, and began walking northwest again.

Daniel scrambled up, looked at Joe Hines and said, "Good luck, mister," and rushed after his father.

Joe gave a casual salute, "Good luck to you good people and your illegal early entry." Joe doubted the Carols heard his parting barb, but he couldn't help himself.

After they put some distance between their brief trail companion, disquiet settled in Robert and Daniel. The green light crept ever closer, and the menacing river's roar convinced them to keep their distance from the river and take their chances in the mist. They only had a few more hours of darkness and shouldn't be able to veer off course by much. Robert hoped to identify a safe crossing point in the daylight and that the patrols continued to stay sparse. Daniel was relieved as they stayed back from the river's edge but kept looking over his shoulder to mark the progress of the green light. As they continued to walk, Daniel's unease shifted to fatigue, and the green light seemed to pause on the river. The light finally dimmed and then disappeared in the fog.

A new light appeared in the east to replace the haunting one. This light was warm and brought first purple, then pink, then red, and finally gold as dawn broke. Daniel was glad for the light but longed to stop. His legs felt numb, and his head was dull from the endless steps. Robert's shoulders ached from carrying the bag of tools and his lower back protested every step, putting him in a foul mood. The sun meant they would have to rest soon, but Robert knew they couldn't until they found a suitable crossing and somewhere safe to hide.

It was two more hours before they found their pass. The water was slower, and the banks of the river eased into the river from both sides, instead of shearing off to an unknown depth. A tall tree had fallen across the river, not enough to make it to the other side, but should the water current grab one of them, they would have something to catch them from going too far downriver. Robert intended to go a bit further, but they needed to save their strength for the crossing, and there were no guarantees that a better crossing would be found.

"We'll cross here after we get some sleep and eat a little. We need to find somewhere to sleep where we won't be spotted," Robert said.

Daniel had a blank look on his face but nodded in agreement. He pointed out a low ridge to their left as if in question. Robert looked in the direction indicated and stared for some time before nodding as well and moving that way. The ridge had a channel on the other side that was formed long ago from water. The ground was a little soft in the channel but would keep them cool while they waited out the sun.

Robert unfurled the buffalo hide and took stock of their tools and supplies. He removed some stale biscuits for Daniel and himself, and he confirmed he had his marking tools. There were some small marking stones, short wooden rods, string, rope, a mallet, a small shovel, rifle ammunition, a few kerchiefs, some food, and a knife with a cross carved into its handle. All told, the pack probably weighed a little over twenty-five pounds with the buffalo hide.

After they ate, Robert wrapped the hide back up and gave it to Daniel to use as a pillow. They lay prone and end-to-end in the narrow ditch, with the soles of their boots opposing each other. Robert took the first watch to keep an eye out for trouble while Daniel slept like one in the grave. While the ground was cool, the sides of the ditch blocked most of the wind, and tall grass waved and rustled on the channel walls. Robert wouldn't be able to hear anyone approach with the noise of the grass but doubted anyone would be able to see the two until they were on top of them. His body was weary, but his mind went to work puzzling out their path ahead. He never saw the lights on the water move by them and he wouldn't be able to tell if the boat passed by during the day. So they had to look for riders in the night as well as watchers on the water.

Daniel slept heavily in the sunshine, but his dreams were dark and strange. He was standing knee-deep in mud, using all his might to take a single step. He heard the yips of coyotes and tried to move faster but he became stuck. The howls and jeers became louder and out of the darkness a lone and emaciated coyote stepped toward him, unaffected by the mire holding Daniel down.

The gaunt coyote opened its mouth and said, "Daniel, son of Robert, lovest thou me?"

For reasons that only make sense in dreams, Daniel replied, "Yes, Lord, you know that I love you."

"Then," said the skeletal coyote, "feed my sheep."

With this, the starved creature returned to the darkness, and the yips died away to a cold silence. Then Daniel heard water rushing behind him and saw the water begin to pool around and flood past him. In the water were the bloated corpses of rodents, dogs, horses, and books unable to close from the swollen pages. They swept by, some catching on him for a moment before passing on and others swirling around in lazy circles. The water kept rising, but Daniel was stuck and couldn't pull free. The water came up over his chin and as he looked to the sky to plead for help. He saw a green moon fill the sky and then heard a thunderous reply to his pleas: "FEED!"

Daniel woke with a start and the sun was high in the sky. He caught his breath and saw his father laying on his back with his hat covering his face. Daniel delicately pushed the supply pack towards his father, trying not to wake him, but his father stretched out a hand and pulled the bag up and under his head without a word. Daniel needed to make water and snuck a glance over the walls of the ditch. He could see the landscape for miles to the south and west. The land was mostly flat, and there were few trees, but the space was filled with rippling grass that moved like water on a lake. It was hard for Daniel to believe that just out of sight there were thousands of wagons gathered, ready to fill the wilderness to the north. He couldn't make out too much beyond the river as the ground rose up, creating a close horizon line. He only took a few steps out of the ditch and relieved himself. He saw some mud on his boots and thought of the dream he had. The details were already beginning to fade from his memory, but the fear remained. He slid back down into the ditch and resorted to stretching his arms and legs with the little room he had.

He remembered he had his book, but he had no desire to read.

Robert didn't fall asleep fast and never slept easy when he finally did. He knew something startled Daniel but didn't say a word about it. It wasn't to spare Daniel's pride or even to respect his privacy; it was simply that Robert didn't care. Who knew what juvenile or senseless things affected that boy? The boy read all sorts of stories and probably put all kinds of nonsense in his head. Robert would provide food and shelter as he must, but he would not entertain any flights of fancy the boy suffered from. Robert fell asleep with his jaw clenched and his brow furrowed. His slumber held no dreams and only a little more rest.

The sunlight disappeared over the horizon and Daniel shouldered the supplies while Robert checked for patrols. They moved out of the ditch and Daniel stepped in horse manure before they made it to the river. Robert noticed and held a finger to his mouth to keep quiet. A patrol must have ridden past while they were still in the ditch.

They made their way up to the river. It was still flowing slowly, but the water was still higher than Robert would have liked. They pulled out their rope and Robert tied it around himself and then around Daniel, not trusting Daniel to make the knots correctly. He pulled it too tight, but Daniel refused to show any pain from the pinch or pressure.

"I'm going to go first to see how deep it is. I will call over once I'm planted on dry land and then you will follow. If you slip, use the rope to pull yourself out. Don't lose the supplies," Robert said.

"I'll anchor myself to that tree up ahead so you can pull yourself out with the rope too," Daniel said.

"Don't let the rope get twisted up when you do," Robert said.

Daniel gritted his teeth at the insinuation that he would get the shared rope caught but before he could fling his own barb, his father turned and walked for the water, raising his arms as his feet became submerged. Daniel hurried to the stump of the fallen tree and angled himself so that the tree would take the brunt of his father's weight, should he need to climb back. Robert's boots filled with water and before long so did his pockets. The water was colder than he expected, and the force nearly swept his feet out from under him. Robert continued deeper until he was forced to give up his feet and swim. The water pulled him toward the fallen tree, and he raised a hand to catch some of the branches and push off of them. He hit the branches hard and felt his feet go past the tree's hanging trunk. Through force of will, he righted himself and brought his other hand up into the tree as well. He wouldn't be able to swim across without closing the gap a bit more. He pulled himself to the end of the tree and then threw himself up and over as far as he could. He landed in the water and quickly went past the tree trunk; he swung his arms and legs as hard as he could and his hand found some roots peeking out from the opposite bank about a dozen feet past the tree. The rope caught in the branches on the end of the fallen tree he'd just pushed off from and now there wasn't enough slack to climb the bank all the way up.

"Daniel, the rope's caught," Robert called over the water.

Daniel heard his father's voice but was unable to make out the words. "Are you ready for me to cross?" Daniel said.

Robert couldn't hear Daniel's response but called out an order, "Crawl out on the tree and free the rope from the branches."

"Okay, I'm coming over," Daniel said.

He followed his father's path and entered the water. Robert, still holding on to wet roots on the bank, spared a glance to see his son's progress on the tree trunk but, in the full moon's light, saw Daniel wade into the water upriver. Robert's blood ran cold, and his mind's eye only saw Daniel strangling himself in the rope and losing the supplies.

"God Almighty! That's not what I goddamned meant!" Robert shouted.

Daniel lost his feet before the water got to his chest, and he was swept straight into the fallen tree trunk. Daniel's head collided with the tree, but his hands couldn't find any purchase in the wet bark. His vision swam and he could taste blood in his mouth. He spit out the blood, but by opening his mouth, he took in the river water to replace it. He started to sputter and choke on blood and water while his body spun and twisted in the current, passing the tree and going into the open river. He came to a sudden halt as the rope went taut from the branches fifteen feet behind him. Robert was shouting for Daniel but couldn't be heard over the water washing over Daniel.

Daniel, unable to focus his vision or get his bearings, leaned on the instructions of his father and grabbed the rope with both hands. He started to pull, hand over hand, moving up the river a few inches at a time. Something washed past him, and he thought of his dream, of the bodies swirling around him, and the water consuming him. His hands slipped and he lost a few inches of progress, but then he wrapped the slack behind his elbow, as if to pull a horse, and stopped his slide. He shook away the specters of his dreams and redoubled his efforts. He pulled himself up to the tree's branches and saw how the rope looped around a branch and went behind him. He turned to see his father hanging on the side of the bank and realized what must have happened. Just beyond his father, Daniel saw a green light down the river.

The light was larger than the night before, and Daniel knew it was coming toward them. Daniel frantically tried to pull the rope free from the branch, but the branch didn't budge and went under the water. Daniel looked to his father and shouted.

"It's stuck, I can't pull it free!" Daniel said.

"Then cut it but keep hold of my half!" Robert said.

Daniel nodded, pulled his knife, and began cutting the rope. The river became more turbulent and rocked as Daniel tried to saw away at the wet strands. Fog suddenly poured in between the branches and filled the top of the river. The water seemed to be rising again, and Daniel felt his feet pulling away from him. Daniel pulled closer to the rope and was working through the final frayed strands when a cacophonous call of coyotes filled the air. It sounded like the banks on both sides of the river were lined with hundreds of them calling and shouting.

"Daniel, cut the damn rope!" Robert yelled.

"I'm trying!" Daniel cried.

Robert couldn't see the critters screaming in the night, but he could see the incoming light from downriver. The light began to resolve into the shape of a steamboat, and Robert noted there was something malevolent in its appearance, but from here, he couldn't determine what. The water was rising, and Robert was worried his grip would soon slip from the roots he held. Daniel was struggling in the water, and Robert couldn't figure out what was taking the boy so long to cut the rope. They needed out of this water before that boat arrived or before the water drowned them. He would take his chances with the coyotes on dry land.

The rope split and Daniel was swept back much faster than before, like something was pulling him by a new unseen rope. Robert tried to pull on the rope to bring Daniel in, but instead, he was jerked free from the bank and joined Daniel in the swirl and roar of water. Daniel lost his knife and sense of direction as the water whipped him about. His father burst out of the fog and linked their arms together. They were nearly in the center of the river, and the water had them high enough that their feet didn't scrape anything under the surface. With nothing to grab or push off from, they just held onto each other and spun in the water waiting to be struck by the boat or drown.

The ghastly green sternwheel steamboat sailed up the middle of the river, its dual smokestacks billowing furious fumes overhead. The boat had a lower deck that wrapped around the cargo hold and was affixed with columns to support the upper deck. The top deck contained an observation platform on the front of the boat that led to a raised cabin from which to steer the vessel. The top deck had metal sheets tacked to it, obscuring the view of who may reside in the cabin. The boat was riddled with holes ranging from the size of a silver dollar to the size of a mason jar. Though there was a green glow coming from the boat, there were whole sections burned to cinders or scored from flames licking up the walls. A dark substance poured down from the bottom deck over the edge and into the water.

The water continued to surge before the steamboat, and as it neared the Carols, the water lifted them and shoved them off to the shoreline. They rode the flood waters over the bank and into the grass before they finally skittered to a stop. Robert and Daniel stumbled to their feet and began untying their portions of rope. The sternwheel at the back of the boat stilled and the smokestacks went dormant. The boat halted on the river, the coyotes silenced, and the moonlight tinged with green. Robert grabbed Daniel by the shoulder and started to run inland. He couldn't accept what he was seeing; perhaps the water in his eyes had disrupted his vision, but wherever this boat came from, it could only spell trouble for them.

Daniel ran with his father and spotted the faint light of a campfire. He pointed it out to his father, but the man shook his head.

"They are either patrols who will send us back, or they are criminals who are as likely to shoot us as they are to help us," Robert said.

A clatter behind them forced them to stop and see the source. A ramp from the boat had been dropped to the ground and now four figures, faintly glowing green, stepped down the ramp in single file. The hair on Daniel's neck raised, and he felt a shiver course through him that was more than the cold of the night. The figures were murmuring amongst themselves and then one stepped forward, raised a rifle towards Daniel and Robert, and fired. The musket round fell a few feet short into a plume of dirt before Robert.

"Seems like we are getting shot either way," Daniel said.

Robert shook his head but resumed running with Daniel directly towards the campfire. That gun sounded like a muzzleloader, Robert thought, not something the army would be using anymore. Daniel couldn't stop staring at the green full moon overhead. Another shot rang out from behind, followed by a raspy shout.

Ahead, the fire of the camp flickered and a large swirl of smoke floated above it, like someone tried to douse the fire with some water. Robert diverted them to the left instead of running straight into the camp. Another shot pierced the earth just ahead and to their right.

The crowd at the smoking campfire appeared to number around a half dozen. They had drawn a variety of weapons, and most were looking out towards the gunfire, but none seemed to notice the Carol boys running by. Daniel assumed their eyes hadn't adjusted to the dark after looking at the light of the campfire. They stayed left and west of the camp and then hunkered down after they passed the camp. Robert unfastened the supply pack and Daniel unshouldered it so they could dump out the contents. They pulled their rifles and swung them to clear water from the barrels. They checked the chambers, pulled back their hammers and lay waiting.

The men of the camp were shouting out at the dark, for one another, and to God. Robert didn't like the look of these men. Their clothing was shabby, but their weapons were gleaming and plentiful. They must be the men Joe was tracking. The hunted men opened fire on the dark and hollered at the top of their lungs. Daniel could see the four phantom-like figures approaching the camp, without slowing, even as the earth around them burst into plumes of debris. So many rounds were fired that the smoke and dirt completely blocked the view of the four or their boat. The camp finally ceased firing and the sound of guns being reloaded and swearing was all that could be heard. Then another gun fired from within the dirt cloud and one of the camp members fell with a gurgling sound.

The four surged through the debris cloud, and now Robert could make out their attire. They were garbed in dark blue caps and coats with light blue trousers that Robert recognized as old Union uniforms, and perhaps because of Daniel's recollections about the scriptures yesterday, when Robert looked closer at these four specters, he was reminded of The Four Horsemen. The first man bore a rifle affixed with a bayonet and had stripes on his arm that indicated an elevated rank. *Conquest.* His skin was swollen and distorted and water poured from him as he walked. The second bore a saber with a red tassel, and his skin was completely gone, as if he had been flayed. He dripped red as he followed. *War.* The third was gaunt and carried a wooden barrel, drumming on the side as he hobbled forward.

Famine. The fourth and final boatman was just a bone-white skeleton in uniform. He was pulling some large ropes, like those used for rigging a boat. *Death*. Robert sat with his rifle ready but not his mind. What more could he do that the bandits beside him had not? What could anyone do?

The slaughter started in earnest then. The four pushed the camp and the living men resumed firing their array of guns in vain. The first bayoneted a man in the shoulder and hoisted him in the air before throwing the man behind him. The second slashed his saber back and forth, hacking off the hands of another victim. The third grabbed one of the wounded and pulled him into his barrel. The man couldn't fit naturally in the barrel, so the gaunt specter repeatedly smashed his hand into the body until it cracked and gushed its way into the unconventional coffin. The fourth unholy ghost caught one of the men by the arm, affixed a rope around the man's neck, and then let go. The rope yanked the man into the grass and his body was pulled all the way back to the boat.

A few men pulled hatchets, knives, and chains and fell upon the saber-wielding corpse. They pressed down on the creature, pushing it into the embers of the campfire, and slashing at the exposed meat and bones. The ghoul ignited from the embers and the men fell back as War twisted and reeled in the flames. The men began to cheer but their glee died as the other three boatmen advanced. The men tried to retreat, but the un-dead soldiers fell on them, stabbing, crushing, and tearing them apart. As another was pressed into the too-small barrel, Famine croaked out, "Fffoood."

The burning boatman took hold of the pos-sessed rigging and was pulled back to the boat. The three remaining spirits approached the final member of the camp with malicious grins. The man had his wrists bound and was rapidly mov-ing them over a small piece of metal. Before the falsely resurrected could reach him, his bonds sheared, he flicked the blade he used into Death and deftly picked up and fired twin revolvers into the boatmen. He ran backwards while firing and jumped up onto a bareback horse, shot the tether holding it, and galloped away from the camp—directly at Robert and Daniel.

The horse reared when it came upon the Carols, but Robert caught the rope just as the bandit fell to the ground.

"Get on!" Robert said.

The horse was large, but Daniel scrambled up it quickly. He took the tether from his father and Robert then pulled himself up.

"Go!" Robert shouted.

"What about that man?" Daniel said.

"No room, now go!" Robert said.

"I bet I could squeeze in," the man choked out while stumbling onto his feet. Daniel hesitated a moment, then recognized him as Joe Hines. His face was battered and bruised but his unswollen eye had the same twinkle as the man they had met the night before.

"Joe! Hop on!" Daniel called.

Joe took the opportunity to hop on the horse and kick it. They took off, riding away from the enraged butchers.

"Hey, let go of me," Robert said.

"I got to hold onto something, and you did steal my horse," Joe said.

They rode on for a few minutes with no clear direction except away from the nightmare they had witnessed.

"Well goddamn, the stories were true after all, huh?" Joe said.

"Why'd they attack us? Do the stories say, Mr. Hines?" Daniel asked.

"Do the dead need a reason?" Joe said.

"Because we're all lawless," Robert said.

"How do we stop the dead?" Daniel said.

"I don't rightly know, but I can tell you what didn't work. Lead, silver, iron and steel were useless. The bullets, blades, and chains didn't hardly slow the monsters. I threw a fine silver dining knife into one of them and they didn't seem to notice."

Daniel thought a moment, then said, "Do the stories say anything about fire? Aside from the first time the boat was burned up."

"Just that some people would light a bonfire to ward off the spirits. That campfire didn't do much to dissuade those ghosts though," Joe offered.

"Your friends doused the fire before they attacked you," Robert said.

Daniel considered his dream, the massacre he witnessed, and what he just heard. He turned the horse around and began riding back to the camp. "I got a fanciful notion."

"What do you have in mind, kid?" Joe asked.

"The *J.R. Williams* didn't sink until it was burned up, and when we just saw it, the only parts that didn't glow green were the parts that were charred. That soldier acted like the campfire hurt it, and you said those bandits had a lot of liquor they stole, right?" Joe said.

"Yeah, that's right . . . enough to make a boat into a bonfire, I'd say," Joe replied.

"The boat will make for tight quarters fighting, and that favors the enemy. We will need to keep them out on open ground where we can keep our distance," Robert added.

"I can keep them distracted. I have plenty of experience with running and gunning," Joe said.

"I know the layout of that vessel, and I can sabotage it with fire. You stay close to me, Daniel, and we can make short work of it," Robert said.

"I can't go with you. There is still one more piece to this and I might be able to fix it," Daniel said.

"What do you mean?" Robert said.

"The Coyote," Joe said, understanding.

"Yes, I saw him. It was a dream, but I think it was more than that. He was starving and asking for food. Maybe, if I bring him food, he will get better. Maybe he can lead the other coyotes away and stop their song from waking the dead," Daniel said.

Robert didn't like this, but Daniel seemed determined, and Robert couldn't discount any piece of this story now. Besides, Daniel seemed to have grasped this situation with more clarity than he or Joe had. "Okay, Joe distracts the enemy, I burn the ship, you help the Coyote."

Daniel, Robert, and Joe found some of the other horses from the camp that managed to break away. The men split up between three fresh horses and rode to the camp site. There they found the aftermath of the attack but no bodies. As Joe promised, there were crates of liquor, jars of oil, lanterns, and some dry rations. Each of them collected their respective items and rode toward the Canadian River.

Three of the boatmen were hauling the bodies to the *J.R. Williams*. The steamboat had some bodies hanging from the smokestacks which began to billow again. Joe rode ahead, pistol drawn, and fired on the three spirits. Robert rode for the ship with crates strapped to his horse. Daniel pushed his horse hard to the river crossing with packs tied to him and his horse.

The three boatmen turned to face the gunfire from Joe. He rode to within twenty feet of them, threw a lantern over their heads, and shot it to pieces with his revolver. The lantern burst into flames over the undead soldiers and the rifleman set alight. The skeleton cast a rope that caught the leg of Joe's horse, yanking the horse and Joe to the earth.

Robert heard the gunfire behind him and the screeching from the undead. He saw Daniel peel off right to where they attempted to cross before. Robert rode his horse straight up the ramp and onto the steamboat. He dismounted from his horse, pulled some of the bottles from their crates, and made his way to the top deck. He started pouring the liquor onto the deck, walls, and even the metal. The door of the captain's cabin opened, and a charred War stepped out with his blade.

Daniel rode into the river, holding tightly to the horse and the covered rations he carried. The horse powered through the current with much more grace than he and his father had. In a few moments, they were on the other shore, and the horse resumed its all-out run. They avoided the ditch he had hidden in before and barreled south into the grasslands. First one coyote called, then another, and then a flurry of calls echoed out, announcing Daniel's arrival but also guiding him. The wind whipped through the horse's mane and tousled Daniel's hair. He felt free, he felt fearless, he felt like he was flying . . . then Daniel landed in the mud. His horse turned over on its back, one of its legs twisted and stuck in the mud.

Joe's horse slid away from him as the rope on its leg pulled it towards the boat. Joe rolled onto his feet and shot the rope that was pulling his horse, and supplies, away. As soon as he stood, the barrel man plowed into him, sloshing gore out all over Joe. The gunslinger, pinned to the ground with the leaking barrel, reached into his pocket and flung ash and embers into the gaunt freak's face. The soldier pulled away and Joe stood once more. Grabbing another lantern from his still-downed horse, he smashed it over the fiend, igniting it, and said with a smirk, "You really thought you had me over a barrel, huh?" A rope fell over Joe's neck and he was suddenly choking.

Robert dodged the saber and cursed himself as he dropped his match. The charcoal warrior spun around and pursued Robert again. The creature's movements weren't as fluid as before. The burned portions of the cadet seemed to wither away, reducing its reach and mobility. "War does that to you, doesn't it?" Robert thought, "it diminishes you." Robert backed into the steering cabin but could not latch the door before the boatman heaved it open again. Robert fell back against the helm, and the wheel ripped free from its rotting housing. Robert grabbed the wheel and struck the boatman, knocking him back. Robert pushed past his staggered foe, lit another match, and dropped it in the puddle of alcohol. The fire spread quickly over the top deck and Robert ran below to ignite the bottom deck.

Daniel pushed himself to a sitting position. His shoulder throbbed with pain and mud covered him. His horse squealed in pain, but it too could not escape the mud. The coyotes gathered in a circle around him and his horse. In front of Daniel, a patch of mud burbled and gushed, and a mangey, withered coyote crawled to the surface.

The Coyote looked to Daniel and said, "Feed my sheep."

"I've brought rations, enough for the whole pack," Daniel said, clenching his teeth in pain.

"I desire sacrifice, not mercy," the Coyote growled.

"The food is a sacrifice," Daniel said.

"The body and the blood are the sacrifice," the Coyote said.

The other coyotes closed in tighter and began to nip at the horse. The horse kicked and cried but couldn't stop their attacks. Daniel, through tears in his eyes, saw coyotes closing in on him. The frail Coyote did not move but only watched.

Joe's vision had gone red. He had precious seconds before his riding days were over for good. The skeleton had wrapped the rope around his neck, put its foot into his back, and pushed. Joe tried to wrench the rope free and tried to shoot the rope, but the skeleton was too strong and fast. In a last-ditch effort, Joe twisted his arm behind him and shot the skeleton's knee. The leg didn't break, but it did turn sideways, and Joe turned with it. As the bone-man slipped, Joe twisted, grabbed the skeleton, and flung him into his burning comrade. The demons squealed in pain as flames crawled across them. Joe, wheezing, pulled the rope free from his throat, and sat back to enjoy the show.

Robert recklessly threw the bottles, causing them to shatter and spray all over the lower deck.

The water beneath the boat began to froth, and the boat teetered sharply. Robert hopped back on his horse and went to light another match. War's burning corpse crawled down from the top deck, raised its head at Robert, and screamed. Robert stuffed a kerchief into a bottle, lit the kerchief on fire, and pegged the demon in the head with it. This was one Union ship he was glad to sink. Robert rode down the ramp as the bottom of the boat was enveloped in fire. He watched the inferno for a moment but then backed away as the river overflowed.

Daniel felt the flood waters begin to pour in, covering the mud and rising on him. They were all going to drown, just like he dreamed. A coyote bit his leg. Another bit his arm. Daniel batted them away, the bites were shallow, testing, but they were getting bolder. The ever-dying Coyote just watched, foam dripping from his mouth, eyes glowing green. Daniel felt something bump into his leg; he looked down, expecting it to be a corpse; instead, he saw his knife, the one he had lost in the river.

"Blood it is then," Daniel said. He grasped the knife and drove it into the devil.

Joe watched the bodies burn until his horse started stomping in place. Joe felt a shallow wave of water hit his boots. He looked down to the river and saw a blazing steamboat sinking into the river. The water around the boat was churning and spilling over the banks. Suddenly, an eruption of green light burst from the river, sending an impossible amount of water in all directions. The light sailed up into the air, spiraled towards the moon, and disappeared. The light of the moon turned white once more, and Joe felt a weight lift from him.

"Godspeed, Daniel," Joe whispered.

Robert was thrown from his horse in the blast of water. He tumbled head over foot for a moment and then found his horse's neck. He pulled himself back onto the horse and directed it to swim south. The flooding was instantaneous, and Robert feared that Daniel would be caught unawares. He pushed his horse and called out for Daniel.

The devil screamed and recoiled from Daniel's attack. The engraved cross on the knife glowed with a white light. The devil's wound steamed and bubbled. The blood that fell on the water sizzled and smoked. The water rose rapidly, and the other coyotes fled the danger. The devil stood on two legs, his green eyes flickering.

"FEED!" the devil hissed.

"Hungry for more, are you? Then have a second helping!" Daniel shouted.

He thrust the sanctified blade up into the devil's jaw, pinning the creature's mouth shut, the blade pressing all the way through the jaw and into the roof of its mouth. The devil recoiled in pain as steam poured from the sides of its mouth. The creature dove into the water and out of sight. Daniel pulled his legs from the mud and stood in the rising water. A hand rested on his shoulder, and he heard his father's voice.

"You did good, son, you did good. Take my hand now and let's be on our way."

Daniel took Robert's hand, and the Carols left the mud, water, and blood behind.

THE TRAJAK TALE OF THE LAST RANGER

BY: TONY GARCIA

For those who came in late . . .

*E*verything we knew ended over 500 years ago. No one truly knows how it all came to pass. No recorded history remains. Now, the sun is barely visible through the perpetual red haze, and freak storms of lightning and hail pepper the landscape. If there are answers, they lie in the wastelands. All that remains is rubble and myth.

It is a new "Dystopian Dawn".

Centuries after technology was destroyed, and the land was still, magic returned. Magic brought by the ancient Faerie creatures who once roamed the earth. Whatever their expectations, they returned to a world blanketed in radiation and chaos. In the ruins of this skeletal world shrouded in deathly twilight, the surviving descendants struggle amidst mutated beasts, monsters, and savages. The landscape lies cluttered with broken remains of a long-dead past. Once-proud cities lie buried beneath centuries of dust and debris. Shadows cast by long-forgotten monuments occasionally break through overgrown forests covered with sickly irradiated vegetation. Long gone are the governments and nations. In their place are fractured tribes and bloodthirsty renegades. Survival of the fittest and rule of the strong replaced any form of democracy.

Creatures of legend once more walk the earth in this new era of super science and magic. Magic and radiation transformed many of the faerie folk and beasts of lore into twisted warped manifestations of what they once were. Treading this ruined world are Mutants, Barbarians, Druids, Engineers,

Scoundrels, and Wizards; all of them battling to carve out a piece of control over whatever this new world will become.

Rarely is anything as it seems. Fallen debris from a shattered moon, wars, radiation, drastic climate change, and shifting tectonic plates created a macabre, dangerous terrain where calm waters can kill and living plants absorb life. Fragments of roads constructed from forgotten materials split the landscape like dying veins. These roads, rumored to once carry vast quantities of goods across the land, are now home to all manner of beasts, raiders . . . and worse. For most, there is no true law—there is only survival.

Merely a few generations ago, the race of Man slowly reemerged. From vaults, shelters, caverns, they came. As Man always does, they set about carving places of ownership. First came the small tribes born of necessity. Those that survived evolved into remote villages. From their humble beginnings, they grew into the provinces and the six major Territories. Built from scraps of the old world, amidst radiated wastes, and designed from the insane visions of what the time before must have been. Into this wasteland of mutants and chaos, the descendants of humankind forged ahead. Each territory was vastly different from one another in appearance, culture, beliefs, and taboos.

Great horrors and wonders lie hidden and long forgotten by all but a select few—those bold enough to uncover the past. These brave adventurers seek out technological and mystical artifacts entombed within the earth . . . perhaps where they belong.

Our tale takes place in the southernmost region of the Alamex territory, where magic is as scarce as water, and laws are made by those with the most guns.

Part 1—Reynolds' Rangers

That was then. This is now.

The sun was high above the black clouds, its rays burning down mercilessly as the two riders approached the camp. Reportedly, the villains they hunted were using an abandoned quarry set in a low valley as their base. Tracking them here was no easy feat—the gang members used different routes, traveling in no more than pairs each time, and did their best to cover any signs of passage.

Sweat rolled down the Ranger's neck as he lay prone, taking in the details of the camp through his spyglass. It consisted of one central location with a dug in burn pit to mask the glow, plenty of vantage points for possible ambushes, and about a dozen small caves at varying heights to hide in. Obscured, easily defended, with more than a few plausible escape routes. It was a smart choice for a hideout.

The Ranger slid a few feet back down the ridge to his companion waiting with their steeds. "I spotted six of them in the open. It looks like they're about to fix breakfast."

"Only six?" Trajak rubbed his chin.

"That I can see. I reckon there are more in those caves yonder. But I can't get a bead on them."

"Trajak not worried."

"I get it, amigo. But these varmints are crafty. We have no idea what to expect."

"Neither do they." Trajak removed two javelins from holsters on his back.

"Whoa there partner, we need a plan. Maybe it's best we reconnoiter for a bit longer before—"

Trajak dived from the rocks, ferociously hurling both javelins in rapid succession. Still in midair, he raised a spear high in both hands and let out a bloodthirsty primal scream. With a shrug and silent curse on his lips, the Ranger ran up and over the ridge, firing shots from his twin Colts to cover his companion's brutal lunge.

Two cowboys already lay dead, javelins sticking from their chests as the robbers scattered under the sudden onslaught. Trajak drove his spear through another villain's chest, showering himself in blood. Two more criminals met the hot lead of justice as the remaining bandit ran for cover in the nearby caves.

"He's heading for the caves to regroup!" yelled the Ranger.

"Trajak see." Wiping blood from his oversized forehead with a gauntleted hand, he jerked his spear free from the corpse with his other hand.

"Partner, Jake has over a dozen members in his gang of thieves. We got lucky. Get ready for anything." The Ranger reloaded his pistols from the bullets in his gun belt.

"Trajak always ready."

"Still, I really think we need a plan this time."

"So, you say." Trajak raised his right hand in salute, then gathered his javelins.

A loud rumbling from above caught their attention. The Ranger raised a hand to shield his eyes from the noonday glare. Squinting to pierce the red haze, he saw a cloud of dust forming from the higher slope. "What in the . . ."

Multiple rifle shots rang out through the valley and a horseless wagon laden with crates and barrels rushed headlong towards them, gathering speed down the slope. Dust billowed up in its wake while black smoke rose from its center. Over the thundering clatter of the wheels a voice barked out at the duo, echoing across the valley. "I see you, Ranger! Time for you to join them other Rangers in hell!"

"Trajak, look out!" The Ranger sprang into action—diving to tackle his companion out of the path of certain destruction. "That wagon is loaded with explosives!"

A few short weeks earlier . . .

Daniel Reynolds woke early, as was his habit. Creeping silently through the log cabin with only the dim slivers of moonlight lighting his way, he made a path for the kitchen. There he struck a match igniting the cast iron potbelly stove. Slowly its dull red glow filled the small room with warmth. While the stove heated, Daniel headed outside, a ceramic jug in one hand and a metal coffee pot in the other.

This was his favorite time of day. Standing on the porch, he watched the sheer blackness of night give way to the rising sun. Its dark orange rays pushed back the night, bathing the land in a blood-colored haze. In between those fleeting moments, Daniel stared between dark clouds, straining to see the few barely visible stars as the landscape went from black to red. It was the stillest time of day. To himself and never out loud, Daniel called it the transition. It wasn't quite morning, and it was no longer night. All was serene in the world.

Crossing the scrub prairie to the pump, Daniel filled both containers with cool water. He spared one last glimpse at the sunrise before going back inside. Setting the coffee pot atop the stove and loading it with medium grade coffee grounds, he mused that one day, when the High Council finally ratified Reynolds' Rangers as an official group, they'd be able to afford the "good stuff".

Daniel's father, Marshall Brett Reynolds, was the next to wake. He nodded to Daniel as he pulled on his boots. Clayton and Jay, Daniel's older brothers, soon followed suit. The three young men all bore striking resemblances to their father. Same chiseled jawline, squint-eyed stare, broad shoulders, and dark hair; Daniel was the shortest at six-foot even. Where they differed was that only Clayton emulated his father's bushy mustache. Jay and Daniel often teased them with names like "walrus" and "soup-catchers."

The other two deputies joined them from the bunkhouse shortly after, conveniently arriving the precise moment the coffee finished brewing. Roger Jackson was a tall dark-skinned man with a shaved head and piercing green eyes. Michael "Big Mike" Irons was the largest of the Rangers, standing nearly seven-feet tall. Where Roger had a wiry physique, lean and cut, Big Mike was a hulking bear of a figure; his gigantic beard added to the effect. The Rangers ate in silence, nodded thanks to Daniel, and went to the porch for a smoke just as the morning sun fully crested the Alamex mountain range.

Without a word, each deputy saddled up their horses and filed in behind Marshal Bret Reynolds. Brett always rode at the front. Their horses were fine steeds, born, bred, and broken at the O'Malley Ranch. Big Mike's horse was the only full trained warhorse, which he named

Smoke. Smoke stood a head higher and two broader than the others—a smaller horse would have a hell of a time hauling Big Mike around. With a nod from Marshal Reynolds, they made their way east and south towards their quarry.

This hunt would solidify them as a special operations group and "Reynolds' Rangers" would officially become the "Alamex Rangers." Currently, it was more of a nickname that started with Brett's uncanny ability to always track down and capture his prey. Today's bounty was none other than the notorious Jake Cavendish Gang. A group of vicious outlaws, wanted for robbery, arson, mayhem, assault, and murder across all three Alamex Provinces.

Brett had a lead and would waste no time in pursuit. He gathered all of his deputies from and around Hellgate for this job. Cavendish was rumored to have a dozen or more men in his band of outlaws, and no one could find their base. They'd normally hit targets located in the wilds between Hellgate, Darwintown, and south towards Boomtown. Stage and rail robbery were their preferred jobs, and they often left stacks of bodies as a calling card. According to his sources, the Cavendish gang had taken refuge in an abandoned mine in the deep nothingness south of Darwintown and west of Boomtown.

After two days and nights of traveling, the Rangers came upon the site. Outside stood several horses tethered beneath makeshift shade but there was no other sign of the outlaws. The glow of a campfire barely illuminated the mine entrance. Marshal Reynolds using hand gestures only, ordered the men to spread out and take up prone fighting positions with overwatch. Nearly an hour passed before they spotted the first sign of human life. A cowboy exited the mine to relieve his bladder and from within the cave came sounds of conversation and laughter. *This* was the right place!

Daniel recognized the bandit as Dwayne "Shifty" Thompson, from his wanted poster. To be sure, he showed it to his father for confirmation. They waited in silence until Shifty went back into the mine. Slowly, one by one, the Rangers crept into the camp forming a semi-circle near the mine entrance. Stealthily, Marshal Reynolds led the way into the den of thieves. The campfire was deeper in the cave than they'd thought and completely deserted. A loud whistle from outside pierced the night sky.

"We've been set up boys. It's a trap!" Those were the last words Marshall Brett Reynolds ever uttered.

Daniel, being the last in line, ran back only to catch a glimpse of Jake Cavendish. The villain laughed loudly as he slammed down the plunger. Explosions rocked the entire mine, blasting the Rangers with fire and debris from all angles. Daniel watched in horror as his brothers were shattered from the detonation. Before he could react, the ceiling and floor gave way, burying them all in broken rock and burning timber. This would be the last ride of Reynolds' Rangers.

Only Daniel survived the fateful ambush, barely and far from unscathed. He fell through the cavern into a pool of buried toxic waste. Near death, his body broken and burning, he crawled from the pool and collapsed half in and half out of the viscous green liquid. Daniel lay in a coma for nearly a week. During that time his body absorbed radioactive energies that somehow miraculously brought him back from death's door.

Waking to find his entire family murdered, he swore revenge upon Cavendish and all evil doers who prey upon the innocent. But first he needed to find a way out of this tomb. Daniel climbed and crawled through the mangled remnants of the mine until a sliver of moonlight piercing through a pile of rocks caught his eye. Slowly, carefully he dug and pushed rocks to broaden the hole. With a glimmer of hope, Daniel pulled himself through the small tunnel, until he was able to reach one hand out into the night sky. He could feel the cool evening air, escape was in his grasp.

That was when the rocks collapsed on top of him, and he blacked out.

Part Two—Enter Trajak

A strange lumbering beast and its rider crested another red-brown cracked dune, the orange sun at their back and red sky high above. The beast resembled a large horse in shape only. Most of its body was covered in thick grey and green scales, its elongated snout sniffed the ground, and its solid black eyes blinked in the heat. The rider was not what most would call "normal" either.

He was a large man with overly broad shoulders and a mop of black hair atop a protruding forehead reminiscent of some prehistoric era. Dressed in torn denim pants patched with leather in places, a black leather jacket with only a left sleeve, a black and green thick hide gauntlet studded with spikes adorning his right arm, pistol belt, and metal-toed leather boots. Across his back he wore a crossed harness holding two crude javelins, a dirty bandana covered his face, and on top of this, mirror-reflective sunglasses shielded his eyes.

He patted the lizorse[1] as it bent to chew sparse grass and roots from the cracked earth. "Beast you can eat now. Trajak eats later. Hrrm. By Hades flaming balls, these ah . . . deadlands must be that place hrrm . . . they call uh, Alamex." His voice has a strange sort of New Rome accent,[2] but with a guttural growl, frequent mumbling

---

1. While horses exist, this strange beast of burden is more common in the wastes. Hardier than the average horse and able to survive on far less water, they are often used as pack animals for caravans. They are easily domesticated and resemble a cross between a horse and a giant lizard—thus the name "Lizorse".

2. By all scholarly accounts, a "New Rome" accent is best compared to that of an impression of an "English" accent, with speech patterns mirroring someone who had watched one too many cheap movies about Rome where all Romans had British accents for some strange reason.

noises, and slow cadence. Reaching in a saddlebag, he pulled out a pair of binoculars that were broken in the middle with only one lens and scanned the horizon. "Hrrm. Trajak sees a valley. It's not far. Hearken to me loyal dumb beast, we go now."

The further inland he traveled, the more the landscape transformed from near-desert to sparse prairie, and the hotter the temperature rose. Patches of darkened grass and stunted gnarled leafless trees gave proof that water of some sort must be close by. Near nightfall, as the blistering heat of the sun gave way to a dull chill and the land was swallowed in blackness, the lizorse became skittish. Jerking its head and scratching at the ground with cloven hooves, Trajak patted the creature's neck to soothe its nerves. "Calm self. Stupid lizard. What do you smell?"

Once more glancing through his half-binoculars, Trajak spotted what must have spooked his steed. He dismounted, patted the beast on its snout, and crept forward a dozen yards without a sound. Just over a low ridge lay the remains of several horses. "Jupiter's nads . . ."

Trajak turned back to the lizorse whispering "Come beast." In response, it scraped its massive snout into the dirt searching for roots. "Hrrm . . . stupid lizard." Trajak walked in a crouch returning to the stubborn beast. After giving it a scolding frown, Trajak gripped the reins and slowly led his mount down into the shallow valley. As he approached, he noticed a large shadow behind the gruesome scene. Horses riddled with bullets, parts scattered across the sand and rock, and dried blood splatters covered several yards. It was as if the horses had exploded. The only things moving were insects swarming the carcasses. Squinting in the darkness as his eyes adjusted to the dim, he was amazed to find the largest horse he'd ever seen, its dark grey coat nearly blended into the nightscape. Calmly and without fear, the animal stared back at Trajak, then snorted and scraped a hoof at the ground.

Trajak advanced slowly, his right hand raised and empty showing the animal that he was unarmed and meant no harm. "Steady horse.

Hrrm . . . steady." This was a magnificent beast, complete with saddle and gear. Silently Trajak thanked the gods Jupiter and Fauna[3] for this gift. Again, the animal snorted and scraped at the ground. Looking down to see what the horse was so obviously trying to point out to him, Trajak saw a pile of rubble. Within the pile, almost invisible in the darkness, was a man's hand.

"All is well, horse. Trajak sees him."

It took Trajak the better part of an hour to uncover the body attached to the hand. Gently, he dragged the man from the wreckage and laid him next to the horse. It snorted and shook its mane with an air of impatience. With his left hand, he checked for a pulse and was more than surprised to find one.

---

3. Denizens of the New Rome territory are raised to believe in the mythos of ancient Rome. While most citizens are far from devout, they do recognize selective holidays and often invoke one or more deities' names for oaths . . . or cursing.

"Good horse. Your master still holds to life. Now shut up."

Trajak set to preparing a small fire and boiling water from a canteen he found on the large grey horse. Among the remains of the unlucky dead beasts, he recovered three more canteens, a few dozen rounds of ammunition, some dried meat, and two wide-brimmed hats, of which he'd never seen the like before.

Donning a black hat, Trajak checked his reflection using his sunglasses, and decided to keep it. "Trajak looks good."

After a short internal debate, Trajak decided not to butcher the horses out of respect. Once the water boiled, Trajak cleaned the man's wounds, and having exhausted his rudimentary first aid skills, propped him up with a jacket as a pillow. The man was young and strong, wearing shreds of denim clothing, black leather boots affixed with spurs, and an empty pistol belt.

His clothing was of no real concern to Trajak, aside from the strange pointy wheels on his boots (Trajak had never seen spurs). Aside from the countless deep slashes, burns, and dark bruising, what caught his eye were the dark green and black veins covering much of his body. They covered much of his back and chest and ran up his neck and across part of his face. In between bites of rations and tending to the living animals, Trajak buried the remains over the hill and away from camp. As he went about these chores, he noticed the green veins on the young man pulsed and glowed frequently for about an hour and then stopped. Trajak was impressed with his own medical skills when he saw that the cuts and bruises had all but vanished. Obviously, the strange glowing veins had nothing to do with it.

"Who are you?" the young man's voice croaked with a slight southern drawl.

"Trajak." He nodded and tossed a canteen to the young man. "Who hrrm . . . are you?"

"Daniel. Daniel Reynolds. Did you . . .?"

"Yes. Daniel, Daniel Reynolds, Trajak saved you."

"My thanks." Daniel took a deep drink. "Why?"

"Huh? Why not?"

"Most folks . . . outsiders that is, such as yourself, wouldn't lend a stranger a hand."

"This is true. Lucky for you I am not those strangers."

"Fair enough. I know better than to look a gift horse in the mouth."

"Why not?" Trajak looked up at the mounts quizzically.

"Just an expression, amigo. I'm thankful for your help. That's all."

"Your horse is great gift from the gods hrrm." He pointed at the large grey stallion.

"Yeah, I reckon he is. Appears to be the only survivor . . . like myself."

"Trajak then is a lone survivor, too."

"You sure do talk strange. What's your story?"

"Trajak has a uh, hrrm . . . story much like any other. I was born . . ."

Born on a forgotten village somewhere between Summerica and New Rome, his mother died in childbirth while Raiders laid waste to his people. The babe would have died soon thereafter if not for the curiosity of Mala. Mala was a great three-armed ape just out scrounging the wastes for food when she heard the infant's cry. It was a strange noise to her ears. Following the sound, another more familiar noise caught her attention—the cackling growls of a hyena pack circling in for a meal! Mala wasted no time destroying the four carrion scavengers with her three great clawed fists. She'd always hated hyenas.

Picking through the carcasses, she found the baby naked and still attached at the umbilical cord to his dead human mother. Having no children of her own, Mala took immediate pity on this hairless monkey with a gigantic head. Aside from his smooth pink skin, he looked very much like an ape. Mala took the babe back to her tribe, most of whom were mutated in some manner as she was. Extra digits, tails, scales, odd fur coloration . . . no two apes truly looked the same. While not pleased with her desire to raise the man-cub as her own, these apes were generally a peaceful lot and having been shunned by their own kind because of their own mutations, perhaps they too felt some small tinge of pity for the hairless infant.

Mala raised him as an ape in their remote village on the outskirts of the southernmost Summerica forests. The name they gave to him cannot easily be translated into human speech, meaning loosely "big-headed ugly man-baby with no hair". Time passed and he grew tall and strong and proudly took his place among the hunters of his ape family. A wild black mane of hair cascaded down his massive shoulders and over his protruding forehead. He knew no other life than this, and despite seeing humans from time to time, he considered himself just another strangely mutated ape.

As all mature apes in their tribe did upon growing out of childhood, it was time for his trial. He was to enter the deep woods alone, survive without the tribe for five passings of the dark, and then return to challenge the strongest ape and take his place as the next great hunter. Sadly, he would never know the outcome of his trial. While away, a far more deadly beast discovered his family—the beast called Man. They came with their fire, their smoke, their loud sticks of destruction, and they slaughtered Trajak's entire family. Heads, fingers, claws, and fangs they took as trophies leaving behind nothing but a burning wreckage. No one would ever know this tribe existed at all.

The man-ape returned on the next day to a horrific scene of carnage and desecration. Slowly and tearfully, he picked his way through the mangled corpses of his family until he found his mother. Mala's corpse lay smoldering, her third arm severed from her body, and a gaping hole in her chest. He cradled his mother's body, rocking back and forth screaming inhuman guttural curses at the night sky. What could wreak such evil? Why? A flock of vultures scattered to the four winds in terror from his screams.

By morning he had buried his tribe and shed his last tear. The time for mourning must give way to revenge. He felt a burning growing inside him that he'd never known. He swore to his mother that he would find those responsible and make them suffer. He'd found large sticks with pointed ends amongst the bodies of the man-things. He would use their own weapons against them. These beasts were careless in their wonton destruction, and it took him no time to trace their tracks. He was of a single purpose now, and no force in this world could stop him.

For three passings of the black he stalked his prey, learning more of them along the way as a good hunter would. They used fire each time they stopped, the warmth of which told him just how close he was to finding them. On the fourth and darkest night, he discovered their campsite. There were six of them. All dressed in strange pieces of animal skins, the like of which he'd not seen before. They danced and laughed around their fire, fueling his anger even deeper. They felt no remorse, nothing for the slaughter of his tribe, his mother. In the shadows he bided on his time. Watching their movements. Waiting for them to sleep.

When only one remained awake, the man-ape struck. From the shadows like a silent panther, he pounced driving the pointed stick completely through the human's chest. Now covered in the blood of his enemy, he stalked them, one by one. Each met death that night by his hands. Two he strangled, another he smashed open with a rock, and the last two he dispatched with his new pointed stick. A blind rage came over him as he tore their lifeless bodies apart, tossing the pieces to the wild for carrion-eaters to feast on. There would be no burial for these beasts!

By sunrise, the deed was done, and he sat cross-legged in the center of their camp, exhausted, panting, and covered in gore. Vengeance was his, but it did nothing to restore the emptiness in his heart where his mother Mala once lived. He had nothing now. No tribe. No enemy to stalk. What was his purpose? He wandered for a few days before bright lights glowed against the black and loud strange noises filled the air. Creeping closer to the light and noise, but always in the shadows, he saw humanity for the first time.

So many humans all in one place. He did not know there were this many in the world! All working together, or so it seemed, dressed in strange skins, crafting things, eating, drinking, speaking their strange language, but not killing each other. Perhaps there was much more left to learn. Perhaps his next trial was before him.

"I would find this place was called hrrm . . . uh, Ashtown. It was in a bigger place called New Rome. So, I hrrm . . . I studied these humans, learn their words and ways, took clothes to look like them, but I would never really be one of them."

"That is the most tragic story I've ever heard, amigo."

"That is what all say when my tale is heard."

"Wait. You're saying that since folks said your story was tragic, you took it to mean that was your name?"

"Yes. I am Trajak." He raised his empty right hand, palm open, in salute.

Trajak hunted for game to eat while Daniel slept. Unbeknownst to either man, the toxic wastes had mutated Daniel at the cellular level. He regenerated all of his wounds, aside from permanent black and green scars covering parts of his torso, up his neck, and streaking to his face. Later, they would discover that when angered, his eyes glowed an unnatural red. Among the oddities, he'd also grown an extra toe on each foot. Daniel kept this to himself.

Within two days Daniel was fully recovered, and during this time he relayed his tragic back-story to his newfound friend. Daniel explained the purpose of Reynold's Rangers, the vile deeds of the Cavendish gang, and what a bounty was. Trajak listened, seeming to accept it all at face value without question.

"Trajak knows revenge."

"It's more than just revenge, amigo. Its jus-tice."

"Hrrm . . . so you say. Trajak accepts this and will help."

"You've done more than I could hope for. I couldn't ask you to risk your life . . ."

"You did not."

"No sir, I reckon I did not. You're a good man."

"This is true. How hrrm . . . will you find them? Trajak is magnificent hunter."

"I pretty much know where their hideout is. We . . . the Rangers that is . . . we were on our way there when he bushwhacked us." Daniel then explained what "bushwhacked" meant, seeing the quizzical blank stare on his companion's face.

"Then we go, and we slaughter them. Easy."

"Well, it ain't that simple partner. As a lawman, I am sworn to bring them to justice. As a son and brother of dead kin, I'm not sure that I can do that. And they know what I look like, so we can't just waltz on in."

"No. Trajak does not, uh, waltz."

"Just another figure of speech. We're not really going to dance." Daniel couldn't help but smile. Trajak was as direct as he was honest. Nuances were lost on him. Perhaps if more people were like him, the world would be a better place.

"Then you must not be you."

"I'm not sure I follow."

"You are dead. You now must hrrm . . . uh, rise from Hades."

"If you mean Hell, I think I get what you're saying. But if I'm not me, who am I?"

"You are the only uh survivor, yes?"

"Yes."

"Then Daniel, Daniel Reynolds, you are now the last of your kind. Own it."

Wearing a hood with eye holes to cover his identity and scarred flesh, Daniel donned a clean set of brown denim pants and a matching cavalry style linen shirt. His pants were tucked into his black cowboy boots with spurs affixed to their backs. Around his waist he wore a black belt for his trousers and a double holstered pistol belt atop this.

In each holster he placed a Colt .45—one belonging to his father and the other his own. Completing the ensemble, he wore a black wide brimmed cowboy hat. Mounting the great stallion named Smoke, he slid his father's Winchester rifle into place. Daniel Reynolds was no more. In his place was a figure who would become a legend across the plains of Alamex. A symbol for order. A terrifying symbol to evil doers everywhere. He was the Last Ranger.

"Trajak! Smoke! We ride!"

Part Three – Hand of Fate

When last we left our intrepid heroes . . .

"Trajak, look out!" The Ranger sprang into action—diving to tackle his companion out of the path of certain destruction. "That wagon is loaded with explosives!"

A burst of flames sent shrapnel in every direction as the keg of powder ignited and the entire wagon exploded. A flaming wagon wheel soared over their heads as the duo rolled for what little cover they could find. Burning shards of wood and metal ripped their flesh.

"Missed me you bastards!" Trajak vaulted over the rocks towards the flaming wreckage. "My turn!"

Trajak dove through the flames both javelins poised to strike. The Ranger rolled to one knee looking for a target. Gunshots rained down from multiple directions narrowly missing the manic charging barbarian. Smoke billowed around Trajak, the burning wreckage behind him only amplifying his primal, demonic appearance. Counting the shots as best he could amidst the mayhem, the Ranger made a dash to his horse hoping the villains were busy reloading.

Meanwhile, above and to the right of the scene, three men took cover to either side of a cave wall to reload their weapons. "What in tarnation?" exclaimed Ugly Pete.

"Shut yer yap and shoot that freak!" is the only answer Jake Cavendish provided.

"Boss, we only got five men besides us. And they is scattered across the hills. Maybe we should hightail it outta here!" Berto, Jake's right-hand man motions with a nod of his head towards the back hills.

"You shut the hell up too! Listen to both of you whining like mules! There ain't but two of them varmints and they're in a damned valley! Ain't no way they make it out alive."

"Three." Ugly Pete took aim.

"What?"

"That weirdo done killed two more. Now there's only three men out there!"

A javelin ripped through the neck of one villain and impaled another through the leg, pinning him in place. Before the wounded man could recover, a deafening crack from the Ranger's Winchester dropped him like a stone. Trajak continued his charge, gripping his spear in both hands. The Ranger, moving from one spot of partial cover to another, took a knee and aimed.

"On your left!"

"What?" Trajak yelled over his shoulder without so much as a glance back. His attention fully dedicated to the cave ahead.

"Blast it! Never mind! Go! Go!" The Ranger put a round through the gang member's chest. Trajak smirked as the dead man tumbled down the hill like a ragdoll to his left. The Ranger pivoted his aim to the remaining gunman on the hill to his right.

"Cover me. I got an idea!" Cavendish holstered his pistol and dug into his saddle bags.

"You got it, boss!" Berto and Ugly Pete shoot down at the rapidly approaching maniac. Berto stood, legs wide fanning the hammer of his pistol, raining shot after shot at Trajak. Ugly Pete fired, still crouched behind cover, his arm cocking back after each blast. Three shots ripped into

Trajak but still he charged on, seemingly oblivious to the pain.

"This boy is plumb crazy!" Ugly Pete couldn't help but laugh.

"Maybe we should recruit him . . . if we live!" Berto joked over his shoulder as he fired towards the charging madman.

"I got this." Jake turned from his bag, a stick of dynamite in one hand and lit cigar in the other. "You might want to duck."

The Ranger spun as a bullet shredded across his ribs. Using the momentum of his fall, he rolled out in the open and rapidly fired three shots up the hill. Trajak never saw the other criminal roll down the hill clutching his chest. What he did see was his target; a man dressed all in black with a goatee that only a villain would wear and holding a smoking stick of dynamite. With all his might, Trajak hurled his only weapon towards the cave nearly fifty yards away.

The spear impaled Jake through his stomach with such force that it ripped right through his back. He stumbled mumbling "What . . . in . . .

the . . ." and fell as the lit dynamite bounced from his hand into the cave.

"Oh sh–!" is the last sound Ugly Pete ever made as the dynamite ignited taking the other six sticks in Jake's bag and the entire cave with it as it exploded!

Trajak sailed nearly a dozen yards carried along with the explosive remains of the three villains and most of the cave entrance. The shockwave carried him back down the hill, showered in gore and shattered stone. The Ranger dropped his rifle and sprinted to his fallen companion

"Trajak!"

Amidst the backdrop of black smoke billowing into the read sky, blood and body parts scattered across the ravine, the Ranger knelt beside his friend. Trajak laid there bleeding from more than a score of deep gouges and bullet holes.

"Not like this. Come on man, you can't die on me now. I can't let Cavendish take another from me."

Helpless, the Ranger looked around for anything he could use to stop the bleeding.

For a brief moment, he thought of dropping his new friend into the pool of waste that gave him his unnatural healing abilities. Scores of random thoughts bombarded his brain.

Could he drag Trajak to the cave in time?

"Come on. Come on, man. Don't do this."

If he did manage to get both of them back into the cavern, would it even work?

"You're too stubborn to die, dammit!"

Even if it worked, could Trajak survive the shock?

Daniel dropped his shaking head in his hands.

"Damn it all to hell! Huh . . . I guess you'd say Hades, pal."

He'd finally gotten his revenge. But was it worth the cost?

"It should be me." Daniel rocked back on his knees and stared into the night sky. How could he justify the death of a good man in his own pursuit of vengeance?

"Damn it, Trajak. You weren't even a ranger!" Was this the future his father dreamed of?

He nearly jumped out of his skin as Trajak violently coughed up a shower of blood.

"Maybe . . . hrrm . . . you were right . . ."

"What?"

"We needed a hrrm . . . " cough ". . . a plan." A thin smile crosses his bloody face.

In the days that followed, the Ranger nursed his friend back to health. Now, both men sat high-backed in their saddles.

"Well, now what?" asked Trajak.

"I plan to take law to the lawless. I vow here and now to bring an end to evil and tyranny in all its forms. No more will the good folk live in fear. Wherever criminals would prey upon the innocent, the helpless, the Last Ranger will be there to stop them."

"Hrrm . . . you need Trajak."

"I wouldn't say no, amigo. There are a lot of bad people out there."

"Sounds fun. Me and my stupid lizard are with you."

They sat in silence watching the Alamex sky slowly turn a deep crimson as the first rays of sun peaked out from behind the mountains. For a moment, the Last Ranger lets a memory of days past slip across his mind. The last ride of Reynold's Rangers. The number of near-death experiences that he mysteriously survived. His strange new friend. Maybe there was a higher purpose behind it all, fate some might say. That was a comforting thought, after all.

With a nod and brief smile, they rode into the wastes, the sun at their backs.

"Trajak! Smoke! We ride!"

This is not The End . . .

BALLADS OF THE PROTECTORS

BY: OSCAR CHAVIRA, JR.

Enrique sits on the edge of his bed, clenching his Bührmann repeating rifle. His wife, Josephine, stares directly at the ceiling of the homestead's master bedroom. Her expressionless, still demeanor hides the fear she carries. The silent night is defiled by the bleating cries of the goats as they are taken by what lurks in the night.

A faint whine is heard in the bedroom as it quickly builds up in intensity. Josephine gasps and promptly gets out of bed to hush the baby that has woken up from the goats' pleas for mercy. The distance from the foot of the bed to the cradle is not far, but the wooden bed frame and the oak floorboards creak loudly with the steps of the frantic mother rushing to calm the baby. Enrique looks back as Josephine's eyes fill with tears while she cradles the baby, hushing the child, attempting to cover his mouth with her hand. The dark bedroom turns a few shades darker. Enrique's eyes widen, and he freezes, watching Josephine's mouth make out the words 'sorry'. Josephine watches in horror as the silhouette of a beast intercepts the moonlight shining through the bedroom window. The tall creature stands on its hind legs, swaying its head from side to side. A harsh, raspy thud comes from the window as the beast puts its meaty paws on the glass. The white curtains hide the creature's features, and in return, the beast cannot see the family within the confines of the structure. The baby feels his mother's rapid respiration, its wails covered by his mother's hand. The baby squirms while Josephine holds him tightly to her bosom. Enrique hears the beast sniffing around the exterior windowsill. He slowly stands up and raises his repeater. The monster's head seems inches away from the window, its meaty paws press against the glass, and the low screeching sound of its claws scratching the glass penetrates the room.

After a few seconds of silence, which feels like an eternity for the family, the creature walks away to continue its meal in the pens. Josephine whispers a lullaby to the baby, soothing him gently. The bedroom door slowly creaks open, and Josephine lets out a sigh of relief and signals the young girl to be quiet with a finger on her pursed lips. Lily tiptoes quickly and hugs her mom's waist; Enrique bends to one knee and kisses his seven-year-old daughter on the forehead.

"Did the goats wake you up?" he whispers. Lily nods. "You're courageous to get out of bed."

Enrique stands up and nods at his wife; she quickly grabs Enrique's arms. "No!" she gently whispers, looking down at the repeating rifle. "At least it scares it away." Enrique pauses and takes a deep breath. "We can't keep losing livestock like this." Enrique pulls his shoulders back. "Don't go," says Josephine. "We've seen that bullets don't hurt it."

Enrique lifts his finger in the air and gently moves it to behind his ear lobe. Both Josephine and Lily perk their necks up, trying to listen. The chaotic rambling of bells and bleating continues. The goats are in a frenzy, watching in horror as a large predator eats one of them in their pen.

"Five times, Josie," Enrique whispers, looking at his wife. "And twice this month . . . we're in the red, we lost our herd dogs. We can't afford to replace them. We can't keep losing goats like this. Whatever that monstrosity is, it has got way too comfortable now."

Enrique slowly walks towards the bedroom door and tells Josephine and Lily to stay put. He creeps down the hallway of his home and gently unlatches the lock to the back door. The light push of the door makes no noise. Enrique's eyes adjust to the night, dimly lit by the bright stars and full moon. Enrique can tell that the stable barn is unbothered; the horses know better than to neigh and make themselves known. The only animals crying out are the goats and chickens, whose coops are right next to the goat pens. Enrique quietly walks down the wooden porch stairs and rounds the corner of the house. He can barely see the black mass of the creature, bent on all fours, devouring one of the goats. The silhouette makes the creature look like a large boulder on the dark horizon; if not for the crunching of bones, the splintering of timber, and the gnawing of flesh, one could easily mistake what lay ahead.

Enrique crouches and gently sneaks forward, ensuring he does not rustle any foliage underneath his house slippers to bring attention to his presence. With a cartridge already chambered, he kneels and raises his rifle. He aims at the boulder-shaped silhouette. Enrique fires two rounds. His fast lever-action speed deters the beast, and he fires a third round. Enrique is stunned when he begins to hear two distinct creatures bellow from the gunshot wounds, but they do not fall. Enrique gasps when he sees two pairs of slightly glowing eyes looking in his direction. Enrique quickly stands up and fires two more rounds before sprinting as fast as he can back up the porch stairs and into the house. He quickly latches the locks and runs to the master bedroom. Josephine is pacing, trying to put the baby back to sleep, while Lily looks tensed, almost as if holding her breath.

"There are two of them . . . now," whispers Enrique, heaving, trying to catch his breath. "They . . . did not run when I fired at them . . . I think they're still out there."

Josephine looks down at her child resting on her bosom and kisses his forehead; she holds the kiss for a few seconds before looking at Enrique. "Are we going to have to move?"

Enrique ponders and walks to his side of the bed. He looks at the oak lamp stand, which has barely visible dust prints from the beam of moonlight coming in through the window.

"We'll see," he says, trying to listen for any scratching from the back door indicating the creatures chased after him.

The chickens could be heard, but the goats' bleating had subsided. Enrique stared at the ceiling, dread overcoming him. *All of this is ruined*, he thought.

The family gets no sleep except Lily, who awakens when Enrique puts on his trousers and boots. Josephine then takes Lily back to her room to continue her rest. Enrique hunches over the vanity, feeling his mouth start to dry up. He makes the promise to his wife that he will ride into town and see if there is anything that could be done. He needs to figure something out, whether it be the sheriff or local men who could lend a hand.

The goat pens are a mess; the creatures were large enough to shatter the wooden structures where the goats lay, and the wooden posts were loose and damaged. The bits of the animals they did not like lay covered in dirt and flies; *ugh, great*, Enrique thought. He moves the remaining goats to the stable barn and thinks about what to do with the chickens since they will be next if he does not do something quickly. He mounts up and hopes to find some countermeasures soon.

Plenty of pedestrians were strolling through the red dirt roads of Yokum. The early trains carrying livestock unload the cattle at the stock show corrals. Merchants are opening up their shops, and Enrique hears the *shink* of one of the butchers sharpening his knives with the body of a freshly killed and drained swine hanging from hooks in his outdoor stall. Enrique pats his mare while he lets a few lumber wagons pass by him; he makes his way to the jailhouse.

"How are ya?" says a young lad lighting a cigarette and looking at Enrique hitch his mare on the hitching post outside the jailhouse.

Enrique greets the young deputy and walks inside to meet with Sheriff Langford. Enrique sees Sheriff Langford mocking a detainee. "Yous thought they were gonna come and help ya out, huh."

The prisoner paces in his cell, infuriated, and spits as the sheriff laughs. Before Enrique can address the sheriff, Langford saunters toward his visitor.

"Enrique! What can I do for ya?" Langford places his dirt-stained cattleman hat on the maple wood desk cluttered with all sorts of papers and coasters used for whiskey glasses.

"Beasts are eating my goats; last night was the fifth time."

Langford brushes his nose with the tip of his thumb and inspects it as if surprised he'd have snot on his finger. "What do you want me to do about it?"

Enrique takes a deep breath and shrugs his shoulders in discontent. "Some deputies, sir, perhaps . . . I've tried to scare it away, but last night there were two. I fired—"

Sheriff Langford raises his finger, interrupting Enrique. "Let me stop you right there." Langford sits on his desk chair. The creaking of the wing doors makes Enrique and Langford look as two men enter the jailhouse with deputy badges on. "You're not the only one, Mr. Monte," Langford continues. "Two months ago, ol' Stroman came in claiming some cattle rustlers had stolen some of his cows. I sent out four of my boys to do a stakeout, hoping they'd catch these rustlers. Mmmm." Langford shakes his head. "It was a whistler the whole time."

The men that had walked in turn attentively, catching something out of context that sparks their attention.

"Are ya talking about the time we lost Joseph?" one of the men asks.

The sheriff nods his head and looks at Enrique. "I'm terribly sorry, Mr. Monte, but I can't send any of my deputies."

The wing doors creak again, and the men see the young deputy walking inside after his smoke break. After a few seconds, Enrique thinks about what he should do since this is his only option. He looks at Langford and asks, "Did y'all kill it?"

"Pardon?"

"This creature, a whistler you call it, did y'all kill it? I wasn't aware Stroman was having his cattle taken, especially from something very strange."

"Oh! Unfortunately, no," answered Langford. "No, haha . . . our bullets deal no damage to foul beasts, Mr. Monte. My men fired at the thing and ran like pandemonium was on their coattails. I've seen Stroman around bringing in some cattle, so I assume he figured out a way to deal with the problem, though."

"I see." Enrique nods and gives a faint smile, turning to the wing doors. "You got a whistler problem?" asks one of the deputies.

"Yeah, something like that," Enrique answers.

"I've heard ranchers employ the services of them protectors," interjects the young deputy. "Shoot, I think that's what that Mr. Stroman feller did."

"You're out of your mind, boy," responds Langford, chuckling while dusting his cattleman hat. "That'll cost ya a pretty penny."

"It's the only thing that works!" declares the young deputy.

While Langford and his men are going back and forth about these 'protectors' services, Enrique makes a faint remark about going to find Mr. Stroman. Enrique leaves the jailhouse feeling disappointed about the lack of help from the sheriff but is curious as to what methods William Stroman has used to deter the problem he has had. Enrique was unaware that other ranchers around the county were dealing with similar issues, although it would make sense. Enrique also admits to himself that it took till the fifth time

for him to come to Yokum to seek help. Mr. Stroman's ranch is about ten miles south of Yokum,
and Enrique doubts he will be in town, so he
mounts up and heads towards Stroman's property.

Enrique can see a herd of cattle grazing in one
of the open fields not far off the road. He halts
his mare, takes a moment, and decides to go and
check if this is one of Stroman's herds. Enrique
lifts an arm in the air, trying to catch the attention
of one of the cowboys watching over the cattle.
Eventually, a rider sees him and trots his horse
to meet Enrique before he gets too close to the
herd.

"You lost, friend?" says the cowboy, spitting a
dark, dense blob from chewing tobacco leaves.

"Are these Stroman's cattle?"

"Why do you wanna know?"

"I'd like to speak to him."

The cowboy spits again while leaning on the
horn and swell of his saddle. "He's at the homestead."

Enrique tips his hat and turns back to the road.
It takes Enrique little time to reach his destina-

tion. He quickly finds the burly man hunched attentively over his tools by the shoeing stock. Both gentlemen dispense with pleasantries. Enrique is abruptly cut off five minutes into telling his story. "Desperation will get you nowhere, Monte. Relax. It's only a few animals," says William Stroman condescendingly while inspecting some horseshoes.

"I got mouths to feed," replies Enrique angrily, having doubts after making the trip all the way to the other side of the county. "Grain, feed, and hay has gone up, price per pound of meat has gone down."

"Don't remind me," interjects Stroman, letting out a big sigh through his nostrils. "Beef has been hit pretty bad, too."

"I just want to put an end to it." Enrique ponders whether he made the right choice of moving to the country and raising animals. "So, how did you kill that whistler the sheriff was telling me about?" Enrique asks after a few seconds of silence.

Stroman heaves and chuckles. "I didn't kill it; the protectors did." Enrique looks puzzled, but before he can ask what or how, Stroman says, "Your parents never told you stories of those protectors and their wicked steeds?"

Enrique takes a pause and thinks. "Not that I recall. I grew up in the city most of my life. And if they did, I probably wasn't paying attention."

"Hmmm, you didn't miss much—just tales to keep us from wandering too far from the property. Well." Stroman starts polishing the horseshoe he was inspecting earlier. "Even in the city, there are things that creep in the night as well."

"I never really paid attention," says Enrique, leaning on the shoeing stock.

"Huh . . . well, my mama used to tell us stories all the time; I never believed her myself until I was fifteen. Let me tell you, Monte, those protectors do their job well."

"How do I get ahold of them?"

"I spoke with that weird sorceress gal Juanita in town."

"The town mage? Really?"

Enrique is skeptical that a local healer would know anything about the creatures that seem to plague ranchers from time to time. Although Enrique himself did not understand them or even know the classifications of different monsters, a local healer would probably know more, depending on what types of wounds people are coming in with.

"Unless you have another way of contacting the order, she's probably your best bet."

Enrique leaves Stroman's property and rides back to Yokum. He is still skeptical and frustrated that his day has been spent on this wild goose chase of finding remedies to deter his problem. What or who these 'protectors' are, he does not know. This is the first time in his life that he has ever heard such a term. Enrique is indifferent about Stroman but also thinks he wouldn't lie about such things. *But if he was lying and I reach a dead-end, then what?* Thought Enrique. *I could use traps and switches, maybe, but I don't think they would hold off those brutes.* He believes he has few options but to talk to Juanita and see what can happen.

"You don't have to explain it to me," said Juanita. The middle-aged sorceress writes on a piece of parchment. "They're an elusive bunch, but word gets around; there are quite a few people who have dealt with the protectors."

The bell atop the door chimes, and a woman leading a boy by his hand walks in, stating that her son drank from the horse trough again. Juanita looks up and adjusts her glasses, and before she could say anything, a young nurse walks through the curtain doors leading to the open ward. The lady and her son follow the nurse, not long after that, an older man with tobacco stains all over his miner's shirt moves the curtains open, limping while pushing a nurse away. "I'm fine! I'm fine!" Repeats the old man. "I promise if I see the bastard again I won't shoot hehe."

Juanita shakes her head and tells the old man that he is not cleared to leave yet. Enrique looks around her clinic; he wrinkles his nostrils with the smell of disinfectant alcohol and bitter fragrance candles placed on every windowsill. The fragrance mixed with the commotion and cursing coming from the ward reminds Enrique of when he interned for a clinic in his younger days. He learned quickly that he was not cut out for that type of job. He found working with animals more serene than working with people.

"I just know the head mage of their order," said Juanita. "When I send her these inquiries, they handle the rest." Juanita smiles, folds the parchment, and seals it with hot wax. Enrique thanks her and heads back home to his wife. *We'll see what happens*, Enrique thinks. *It doesn't feel like I have done anything, but at least a few people know of the problem.*

The next two days and nights are silent in the Monte ranch. The family tends to what needs to be done on the property and worries if the night will be the night that the brutes come back to feast. A few more days pass; Enrique continues with his work and rides into Yokum for supplies and feed. Juanita tells him there is still no response. Enrique wonders if his message ever reached these 'protectors'. Soon, a whole week passes. Although the week has been peaceful regarding the monsters not returning, he worries now about the inevitable and the help that should arrive at any time.

On a warm, beautiful day, dusk arrives, and the family prepares for the night. Around midnight, they are awakened by a booming knock at their front door. The baby is frightened and begins to wail. Josephine quickly picks up the infant while Enrique charges down the passageway with rifle in hand. Another booming knock rattles the door and the frame.

"STATE YOUR BUSINESS OR I'LL SHOOT!" roars Enrique, pointing his repeater at the door.

There is a brief silence before a voice is heard from the other side of the door. "You da feller with the beast problem?"

Enrique's eyes widen, and his shoulders lower slightly before he tightens his grip and takes a better stance. "Is this some kind of joke?" Enrique's voice is taut.

"No sir," responds the gruff voice on the other side. "Just trying to do our job."

"Get lost, friend! Not at this hour!"

After a few seconds of silence, the voice states, "You can go back to bed, Mr. Monte. We'll patrol the area."

Enrique hears heavy boot steps walking away from the other side of the door. He thinks about slinging the door open and firing at whoever is trespassing, but he quickly remembers who he has been expecting. *At this hour!* Enrique thinks. He stops himself from doing such a thing in fear of inviting some malevolent spirit into his home by giving it easy access through the front door. He tiptoes back to the master bedroom and informs his wife of what just transpired.

"This is scaring me!" whispers Josephine. "What are we going to do?"

"I-I don't know, I guess this is our help . . . I mean," responds Enrique with an uncertain look on his face of wanting some approval from his wife.

"I don't think this is specifically what you asked for!" An unpleasant reaction is warranted from Josephine, as both hear that something or someone is roaming their property without their permission. Enrique creeps to the bedroom window

and peers into the night. He sees two lights swaying from side to side—lanterns around the goat
pens. Josephine sneaks behind him and asks if it
would be wise to do something about it or let this
pass.

"I have no idea what is going on, honestly. The
fact that it knew our surname . . . I don't know."

Enrique continues to observe the lanterns
roaming around the goat pens and the chicken
coops, and the light radiating from them allows
Enrique to pick out a few details. They are hu-
manoid in shape, with two legs and arms; he
cannot get a glimpse of their upper bodies. The
lanterns lower and rise, indicating the persons
holding the lanterns are crouching and standing
up. Enrique does not hear any clinks or loud
bangs suggesting they are trying to steal farm
equipment. He sees one lantern walking away
from the other; Enrique tries to follow it and
stretches his neck as far as the window allows
him. In the distance, the lantern stops by a horse.
Enrique can make out a saddle bag; he imagines
someone rummaging through their saddlebags
for supplies.

The lantern gleams around its surroundings; the faint swaying from its slim handle illuminates the rear end of the mount that Enrique imagined was there. Though Enrique cannot quite fathom the picture in his mind. To Enrique's eyes from afar, there seems to be little muscle on the horse's hindquarters, but more peculiar than just skinny or sickly. Where the rear end of the mount should be, there seems to be emptiness, hollow spaces surrounded by opaque cream.

Bones! Enrique thinks to himself. *It's the night, the lantern, the window . . . Yeah, I just, huh*? Enrique reasons with himself and continues to observe over the next half-hour. Nothing extraordinary happens. Enrique sees the lanterns doing the same thing: walking around the property, stopping in certain areas, observing, and continuing to walk. The low adrenaline and the song of crickets and cicadas make Enrique drowsy. Josephine falls asleep with their child in the rocking chair. Enrique gets away from the window, kisses his wife on the forehead, and plops on his side of the bed.

The next day, Enrique walks diligently around his property and notices nothing is amiss. Whoever they were with their lanterns, they did not move any of his equipment, and no animals were missing.

He continues doing the work he needs to do throughout his day; Lily follows him around, imagining she is helping a great deal with the heavy chores. Her playing and twirling a lasso ceases, and she mentions, "There! Right there, Daddy, look."

Enrique stops brushing his mare and steps out of the barn to see, in the distance, about five hundred meters to a kilometer away in the prairie, two silhouettes: riders hunched over on their mounts. They spur their horses and trot a bit; Enrique sees them glaring in his direction and gets a good view of the profile of the steeds.

"Get inside, sweetie," says Enrique sternly to Lily. Enrique squeezes her shoulders and pats her on the back, urging her to hurry to the house.

Enrique hides his awe from his daughter while she returns to the house. He strains his eyes to get a better view of what he recognizes as the feeble, lanky creature of one of the riders. Both riders are wearing regular attire, apart from one wearing a duster coat. Enrique makes out a rifle butt from a saddle scabbard. The mounts, however, Enrique is confident of what he witnessed the night prior. Decaying flesh holding on tightly to thin tendons hanging like feeble flowers in the wind, the discolored cream foundation of the legs and parts of the ribcages lead no doubt in Enrique's mind that they are undead.

He sees them ride off into some mesquite brush encompassing the prairie and disappear. Enrique becomes jumpy after that and even slings his repeater across his back for the remainder of his work day. Enrique and Josephine are awoken that night by the bleating of goats being driven from the barn.

"No!" Enrique exclaims. "Bastards!" He quickly puts on his boots, grabs his gun, and starts to run toward the door. He stops for a bit before opening it thinking about the lack of damage he has dealt to the beasts, but his resolve does not let him back down. "HEY!" he screams, unable to see which direction he needs to shoot at.

A young man about the age of twenty, fair-skinned with dark circles under his eyes. He wears a black wool cattleman hat and two bandoliers strapped in an X across his chest. He approaches with his hands up from the darkness.

"Ayyyee easy now, Mr. Monte."

Enrique's complexion turns pale, and he takes a step back. "Who the hell are you?! What are you doing with my goats?"

"We need bait," another voice resonates, coming from another young man as he appears from the shadows. He is the same age as the one Enrique is pointing his gun at; his face is more rounded and has a burn mark on his neck. He was wearing a duster coat and a double-barreled shotgun slung across his back. "We don't know what's been killing them, so we need to draw this creature out."

Enrique continues to breathe frantically and with the butt of the rifle steadily pressed on his shoulder.

"Relax, Mr. Monte," said the one wearing the duster coat.

"How do you know my name?" Enrique points the gun back and forth at both men.

"It's what was on the contract we received. Mr. Enrique Monte, is it not?"

"Y-Y-Yea, and what contract? What are you talking about?!"

"We're protectors, just doing our job."

Enrique lessens his grip but still points the repeater back and forth to the two gentlemen.

"It's late, why now? I never permitted you to be here," said Enrique before remembering his talk with Juanita.

"We can discuss this after we're done, Mr. Monte."

The two men turn their backs on Enrique and continue to push the goats to the pens. "We advise you to go back inside," said the lad with the black wool cattleman hat and the two bandoliers strapped in an X across his chest. "We still don't know what we are dealing with here."

Enrique is speechless but will not be deterred. "I don't care! Leave!" exclaims Enrique. "I was under the impression that protectors were professionals, not men who show up in the middle of the night. Now get the fuck out!"

"We're professionals, but we're certainly not those kinds of 'professionals'," chuckled the other protector wearing the duster coat. "The letter we received said you had a big foul beast eating your livestock, so that's why we are here."

"What we found certainly ain't no coyotes," remarked the one wearing the bandoliers. "But we'll have our answers here pretty soon." The protector points out in the distance. "We are being hunted right now."

The one in the duster coat remarks, "Mmmm, what do you think? An ughal?"

"Nawww," responds the other protector, unholstering his revolver. "Doesn't have red eyes."

He clicks on the ratchet of the cylinder, and six cartridges jump out. Enrique sees him whisper something inaudible. The cartridges glow a bright red and then subside in their illumination. The protector loads his revolver again and closes the break action.

"We implore that you go back inside, Mr. Monte," the round-faced protector says in a more serious tone. "You'll only get in the way, and we will compensate for any goats lost."

"W-wai—" utters Enrique while being slightly pushed by the other protector to go back inside.

"Lock the door; we'll let you know when we're done."

Enrique watches as his goats enter their pens without fuss, and the two protectors stride ahead, giving each other different hand signals. *What just happened?* Enrique thinks to himself. He decides to heed their words, goes inside his home, and locks the doors. He does not trust what is going on, but he also does not question what he witnessed when those cartridges illuminated bright red.

Enrique informs Josephine of what happened.

"I mean, is this what you imagined when Mr. Stroman told you about these protectors?" Josephine asks.

"I was hoping there would be more clarity," responds Enrique, peering through his window, trying to keep an eye on his animals. "All of this is too confusing."

The usual sights and sounds of nighttime are present; Josephine checks on Lily and tries to get rest, feeling safe that her husband is watching through the window. The silence is quickly broken with the echo of a gunshot. Enrique estimates it came from a couple hundred meters away from the house. He remembers what was told to him about being informed once these creatures were dead. The gunshot raises the thought that perhaps that was it, just two hunters killing their prey.

A loud thud suddenly sends a jolt through Enrique's spine. The thud comes from the roof, like something landed on top of the house. Josephine startles and screams; a strange raspy noise follows the thud like a sharp pick scraping on stone. Enrique follows the noise with his eyes, trying to deduce what it is.

He suddenly hears a faint yell outside, "Where did the other one go?!"

Where did it go? he thinks. He pulls the curtains to the side to see outside. He lets out a yelp and jumps back; a large mass leaps from the roof. Right in front of the window stands a menacing creature about seven feet tall. It is sniffing, pacing closer to the window. Enrique cannot look away at the brute; this was the closest he had ever seen one of the beasts. It is alien to Enrique; he has never seen such a creature with dark coarse fur throughout its body and with a bumpy reptilian-skinned face. There was something unexplainable in Enrique's stomach, as if a little voice was telling him that what he was seeing was not of this plane of existence.

Enrique freezes as he makes eye contact with the monster while it is sniffing the air; the beast moves closer, peering through the window at Enrique. Its hot breath fogs the glass; its heavy furry paws press against the window while the claws give that distinct screeching sound that Enrique has heard before. Another gunshot, and the creature bellows and turns its head to the direction the shot came from. More gunshots are heard, and Enrique flinches as he can feel that a few hit the house.

His wife yells; he musters the confidence to move and grabs his repeater. "Come on! Come on!" Enrique grabs Josephine. "Take the kids! Up to the attic or something, lock the hatch!"

The creature continues to stand on its hind legs and turns its attention back to the commotion inside the house. Enrique sees the monster's pupils dilate and nostrils flare immensely, as if driven by bloodlust and fear from others. It puts all of its weight and might toward the window of the master bedroom. With sheer force, the brute breaks the glass . . . a loud crash, yelling, and a low bass howl penetrate Enrique's ears. He reacts and fires his rifle at the window. The bullets offer little resistance, the beast persists despite being shot at. No blood oozes from its hide. Josephine grabs the baby quickly, which starts to wail, and runs out of the room yelling for Lily. Enrique looks at the beast as it pulls its body through the window frame. A large furry monster with strong muscular hind legs and canine-like paws. Then there is a battle cry behind the creature, and it sprawls over. Red streaks and little puffs of smoke come from the monster. Enrique tries to keep his composure and sees through the window frame that one of the protectors is firing at the beast. The red darts from the revolver disappear in an instant to the naked eye, but still, the bullets from the protector have little to no effect on it, just like Enrique's repeating rifle. The creature gives a loud howl towards the protector, it shakes itself like a mutt, leaps away from the window frame, and rushes at the protector at full speed. Enrique witnesses the beast tackle the protector and swipe at his chest while the protector pistol whips the monster. The creature suddenly stops as it is hit in the upper back close to its neck.

Galloping and hollering become more apparent, and Enrique sees the round-faced protector with the duster coat rush to the scene, riding his undead steed. The grotesque body of the lanky entity, which once was a horse, rears itself and bucks at the furry beast. The rider fires more shotgun shells. Meanwhile, the one who was tackled rolls on the ground and pulls himself up, firing his revolver at the monster. Both unleash a volley of rounds, but the beast refuses to surrender.

"Continue to use acid!" Enrique hears from the protectors.

"Nothing is working, dammit!"

"Where's the other one?"

"I lost it . . . it ran off!"

After that remark, a loud howl is heard through the loud pops and whistles of the bullets, but it is not from the beast that was being fired upon. Through all the chaos, Enrique's ears perk, and a cold sensation runs down his spine as he hears Lily and Josephine screaming from somewhere in the house. He does little thinking; his body reacts without him processing what is going on. His legs take him to his daughter's room while he yells for his wife and kids.

Entering his daughter's room, he sees what has made his family scream. The other creature pushes against the glass of the window and shatters it.

"Get behind me!" Enrique orders. He fires his repeater, hoping that it will stop the beast from trying to jump in through the window frame. After firing three rounds, he quickly loads more cartridges into the repeater and tells his family to run.

The beast does halt when fired upon, but promptly regains its poise and starts advancing. Enrique runs out of the room and closes the door behind him.

"Run! Just run!" he yells, his voice muffled by a loud thud and furniture breaking against hardwood flooring.

Enrique looks behind him and sees the wooden door break while the brute sniffs the air before targeting the running family. Josephine unlatches the front door and grabs Lily by her arm. Enrique continues to fire rounds at the beast while it makes its way through the hallway passage. With no time to get up to the house's attic, the Montes break for the outside.

"Just run!" yells Enrique, watching his family bolt through the darkness and harsh foliage of the dusty plains.

Enrique turns around every few steps, hoping not to run into the protectors and the other monster. He sees the beast continue to advance on them and keeps firing at the beast, ensuring he holds it off while backpedaling and continuing his movement. The protectors continue to fight the other beast, unaware of the one chasing the Montes. Enrique fires all the rounds from the repeater and continues to sprint; he is unable to reload on a sprint and decides just to run. Adrenaline forces his body to keep pushing despite his harsh breathing and tiredness. He catches up to his wife.

"Give me Lily! I can carry her!"

The young girl extends her arms and grabs her father's hand. He flings her on his back. He can feel her tense arms slowly choking his neck, but he continues to push. Lily's crying and heaving by his ear blocks out the low howl right behind them. Enrique finds an extra boost in him as he almost feels and smells the hot, foul breath of the beast.

In a moment of hyper-fixation on just running, his mind blocks out all surroundings, his sight becomes blurry, and a warm sensation trickles down his back. A warmth that, for a moment, brings bliss as the cool wind breaks against his face. His stride falters, and he notices the once-tense arms of his beloved child loosen. The screaming of his wife seems almost distant; the hard dirt that brushes on his face as he topples brings his mind back to the inevitable. He rolls on the ground and his body reacts. He quickly picks himself up, although his mind has dissociated. The smell of iron fills his nostrils, and the warm water he felt trickle down his back becomes apparent. His daughter, squealing and full of blood, squirms on the dirt and grass. The beast was able to slice her back, and a huge gash paralyzed Lily quickly.

Without rationality, Enrique grabs the barrel of his repeater and twists his torso, using the gun as a blunt melee weapon on the head of the beast inches away from the girl's face. The reptilian face and maw of the beast roar at Enrique while taking the blows of the weapon, but Enrique's efforts are in vain as the creature lowers its head, only focused on the prey below it. A loud crunch and a splatter of red sounds the victory for the beast. Its powerful jaws crunch the skull of a child with ease. Enrique continues to bash the monster's face with the butt of the rifle, but the beast swipes at Enrique toppling him away with its massive forearms. He hits his head on the dirt and rolls awkwardly, forcing his body to contort in uncomfortable positions. While trying to get his bearings, the beast then lunges at Josephine.

Josephine tosses the infant toward Enrique's direction in a last effort to save her child in a motherly sacrifice. Enrique yells, watching Josephine be disemboweled by the monster's dagger-like claws. Her screams turn to gurgles as she drowns in her blood. Enrique uses all his might to lunge on top of Lucas, hoping that what is about to happen will happen quickly. The monster, in frenzied bloodlust, swipes at Enrique's back. The sharp, stinging pain lasts only briefly before it ends from nerves being severed. Enrique's body releases its bowels while his mind only wonders about the safety of his child, and he whispers, 'I'm sorry.'

"It's over here!" says one of the protectors, both whipping their undead steeds as they approach the unfolding carnage. The creature gives an agonized howl as its flesh begins to transform into an icy form. Both protectors fire relentlessly at the beast, finally having figured out what type of ammo can kill these types of monsters. Its slowly freezing flesh halts the monster from trying to run. The shotgun slugs encompass the monster's entire body; its howl slowly decrescendos. What was the beast moments ago is now a solid block of ice that starts breaking down into small pieces. A fierce fire engulfs the monster, giving the protectors a sigh of relief, knowing that they killed it. A fire with no smoke, signaling that this, indeed, was a soulless wretch.

Both men dismount their horses and check on the family.

"Poor woman," said the protector wearing the bandoliers while closing the eyes of Josephine.

"Geeze," the round-faced protector rubs his chin and wipes his forehead. "We were sloppy."

They hear the muffled wailing of the baby, it is faint but audible. One of them quickly searches for the child. He flips the limp, lifeless body of Enrique.

"Baby is alive!"

"Well, pick it up, damnit! We'll take him with us."

They see the remains of the little girl. "All dead. This is not good," says one of the protectors, checking the wounds of the deceased.

"I wonder what its name is?"

The infant wails while the protector tries to soothe it.

"We can always check the records for the family in the courthouse. That won't be too difficult," says the other protector in the duster coat, gathering the creature's ashes into a small vial.

"It has a bracelet, with a little bit of light—hold on." The protector carries the child and holds him close to the lantern's light. "I think his name is Lucas."

"We'll take him . . . he'll be our payment for this contract."

"The Order isn't going to be happy with this one; it was pretty sloppy and cost some lives."

"Mmmm, it's part of the job. At least we were able to save one." The protector wearing the duster coat glances at Lucas, the child still wailing. "He'll tire himself out . . . congratulations, little guy. I guess you'll be part of our guild."

The protectors gather the bodies and place them together to make it easier to find them among the prairie grasses. Civil twilight begins, and the stars illuminate the horizon with a beautiful pale blue sky.

"This will be easier to let the coroners know where we left them," one of the protectors says while placing blue bonnets he plucked nearby on top of Enrique's body.

Lucas, tiring himself out slowly, starts closing his eyes. The protector holding him whispers, letting him know how bravely his family fought to keep him safe.

Both men mount up their undead steeds and ride off to report back on the completion of their contract and for the bodies to be given a proper burial.

SNAKE OIL

By: George Cottonwood

1

The sun was high, oppressing everything beneath its heavy heat. Smart creatures found shelter underneath rocks or in the roving shade of a juniper. They waited till dusk to run their errands in the cool of the evening. As a general rule for survival, they did not do what Lieutenant Dusty Thorngage was doing: riding in the hottest part of the day through the arid plains of Sumadea.

Dusty removed his wide-brimmed hat and wiped the sweat from his face with a bandana.

He knew better, but he hadn't much of a choice in the matter. He had to ride because if he didn't chance upon water soon, he would be in trouble anyway.

As a light cavalry officer in Breckenridge Falls, Dusty insisted his rangers carry at least two days' worth of water. However, when you are ambushed, and an enemy arrow has punctured one of your canteens, you don't have a lot of choices. Thankfully, he had a second canteen, believing in another rule that "two is one and one is none."

He took a careful swig, steadying his tired hands so he wouldn't spill any water. He was traveling back from a brief assignment with another ranger troop to the southwest of Breckenridge. They had been chasing raiders out of the interior, and it had been a dangerous mission. Now he was pushing to make it back to Breckenridge by morning.

He plodded alone on his mountain pony named Amigo. Dusty was a halfling and rode more comfortably on the smaller steed. Cob ponies were bred for mountain trails and herding, but Amigo did well at any work Dusty put him to, though the heat was affecting him too. Amigo hung his head low as they continued their steady pace through the crispy grassland.

They climbed a small hill, hoping to see the welcome sight of the town from its top. The wind played tricks on his ears; he thought he could hear shouts carried along as the air blew past him.

Rider and horse paused at the hill's highest point. Dusty could see for miles in every direction, the mountains ahead and to his right and the silver glint of the coast behind him. He also saw that the wind hadn't been playing tricks on him; it was delivering a distress call. Below into the next valley, he saw a large, garishly painted wagon, pulled by two donkeys and driven by a figure in a large hat, veering wildly as it attempted to evade four riders pursuing it.

He cursed softly and spurred Amigo towards the fracas. He had a light crossbow slung across his shoulders by a rope which he pulled around for quick access, securing it on the saddle horn. He loaded a bolt and cocked it.

As he approached, Dusty discerned the wagon's garish lettering—Gente and Verrel's Miracle Elixir—in eye-straining pinks and yellows among a clash of greens, yellows, and reds. The four riders were full-size, but he couldn't tell if they were human, orc, or elf.

They were all headed for a dry streambed and the wagon would need to slow down to cross it safely. Someone wearing a hood popped around the passenger side of the wagon and fired off a crossbow bolt at the lead rider. He jerked his horse to the side and the bolt barely missed him, scratching his side.

Dusty closed in on them. Amigo was breathing hard at the chase work. Dusty was within a few yards of the rearmost riders when he started shouting, calling them to halt. The two in the back whipped their heads around to look at him, and Dusty saw one was a human and the other a half-elf. He called out again, but they ignored him, instead calling to their friends in front of them, who also turned and looked at Dusty. These were two stout-looking men, and they glared at him before turning back.

The hooded figure popped up from around the front of the wagon and Dusty thought it might be a woman. She braced against the top of the wagon and fired her crossbow again at the rider closest to the wagon. This one stuck him in the leg, and he cried out before pulling away and falling behind. Dusty saw the woman look at him for a few seconds before disappearing again.

The wagon slowed as it approached the streambed, allowing the remaining riders and Dusty to close the distance. Dusty rode up to the rider nearest him, leaned over, and smoothly unlatched the bridle from the horse. The rider was forced to slip away, and he loudly cursed the halfling. Dusty rammed Amigo into the side of another rider, and Amigo took a bite out of the horse's flank, causing it to rear up and fall back.

That left just one, the half-elf. He was staring over his shoulder at Dusty now. Dusty raised his crossbow and jerked his head to the side, signaling to break off the attack or risk getting shot. The half-elf glared, then gritted his teeth and steered his hoss off the road before turning around and, ending the chase.

Dusty replaced his crossbow across his saddle. The woman appeared again and looked around. Dusty held both hands up with palms facing out. The wagon continued to slow its pace while the woman stared at Dusty, occasionally speaking to the driver whom he could not see. She waved at him, gesturing to the driver's side, and then disappeared again.

Dusty obeyed and rode Amigo up the left side of the wagon, approaching the driver. He saw a man wearing a tall hat with a narrow brim and a gaudy peacock's feather stuck in the band. He smiled at Dusty. Past him, Dusty confirmed the passenger was a woman. She was wearing a light cloak with a hood over her head to protect her from the sun. She was aiming down the sights of a crossbow at him. The driver winked.

"I'm with the rangers," Dusty called out. "Those other fellers stopped the chase. You're alright now."

The driver, still smiling, reined his donkeys to a halt. The woman lowered her crossbow, revealing more of her face and eyes, and Dusty could see that she was stunning. She had long, dark hair spilling out from the hood. Her green eyes were small but sharp, and she had a petite nose and red, red lips. Dusty stared, and she stared back as they stopped.

The driver introduced himself with a flourish as *Monsieur* Gente, and his companion was *Mademoiselle* Verrel. They were traveling merchants, selling "the most wonderful and miraculous cure-all" from town to town. They had been making their way inland from the coast when they were waylaid by the four riders Dusty had "heroically defeated." The woman did not speak but continued gazing at Dusty, who found it increasingly difficult to look away.

Gente offered Dusty a flat, green bottle. "Thirsty? Try some of our elixir. It's sure to quench the worst thirst and relight the dampest fires," he said.

Dusty felt his dry mouth with his tongue and took the bottle. He pulled the cork with his teeth and took a big swig. The liquid was light and delicate, sweet with a hint of anise at the end. It was not unpleasant or medicinal in the least.

"Thank you," he said after taking several more pulls from the bottle.

Feeling refreshed, he recorked the bottle and handed it back to Gente. He felt light-headed from the hard ride and lack of water. Perhaps it was the tonic. Or maybe it was the enchanting stare of the beautiful woman named Verrel, who never seemed to take her eyes off Dusty's, peeking out at him from underneath her hood.

"No, no. That is yours, old chap. A way to say thank you for your assistance. Where are you headed?" Gente asked cheerfully.

Dusty was feeling numb, but at least he was less thirsty. He continued to watch the hooded woman while he answered. "Breckenridge Falls. It's that way," he said, pointing ahead of them without looking.

"Why, by happy fate we too are headed for Breckenridge Falls. We would be obliged if you escorted us the rest of the way," Gente said.

2

It had been three days since they arrived in the frontier town. People buzzed through the streets like bees in spring. Everyone wanted to see the newcomers and watch their show, put on each night as part of their act for selling their strange elixir. Gente would perform minor tricks and illusions combined with jokes, then he would demonstrate the effects of their elixir by using it as a salve for scrapes and bruises or by removing stubborn stains from a tunic.

But mostly the elixir was touted as a daily preventive against colds and illnesses. "Better than your momma's fire cider, a sip of this a day will keep any disease away," Gente said. On most nights the lady Verrel would sing and play a harp. Her voice weaved and wound itself around her listeners, whispering and promising. It was this more than anything that sold bottles. When the townspeople listened to her sing they felt like they could wrestle a bug-bear and date its sister. Women felt high-born and men felt brave and marvelous, feelings somehow encouraged by sipping the cloudy elixir.

After a show, if the two newcomers were in one of the two saloons in town, then the other was empty. The pair were favored amongst the townsfolk, Verrel more than Gente, though this didn't seem to have bothered him at all. He almost seemed to encourage it. At a dance the town had hosted, Gente allowed anyone to ask for Verrel's hand for a dance. He would laugh warmly, while she would smile a sweet smile from behind a veil that half covered her face, batting her glinting green eyes.

Maybe it was the heat of the season, the pressing of the crowded taverns, or the strange desire to show off and perform before the cloaked lady, but more and more fights were breaking out, even amongst friends. The shire-reeve, a tall man with a handlebar mustache named Orrin Shackleton, was busier than ever trying to keep the peace by breaking up bar fights in an otherwise friendly town.

Even Dusty was challenged to fight in one of the crowded saloons one night. Normally, he would have patrolled around town until late in the evening when he would retire at the ranger barracks. But lately, he had been spending more and more time in town in the presence of the two visitors. That night they were in the Wary Sheep Saloon.

And so was Beau Carson. Carson was a hand at one of the ranches a few miles outside of town. He was considered a top hand, having the experience and skill to reliably drive livestock and organize the day-to-day work on the ranch. They were friends; Dusty had always gotten along with him and respected his work ethic. However, that night Carson was drunk on the miracle elixir mixed with whiskey and was surly and unhinged.

While Carson had been refilling his drink at the bar, another person had been invited to take his seat at the table where the lady Verrel was sitting. It had been a halfling, and it had not been Dusty, but Carson was too drunk to be able to see the difference. Finding his seat occupied, he sulked back off to the bar, seething with the frustration he felt for his failed plans of grand gestures. Carson was so focused on his drink that he had not seen Dusty walk into the saloon until he had climbed a stool next to the ranch hand and flagged down the busy bartender for a drink.

Carson looked down at Dusty, staring with red eyes. Dusty flashed a smile and then turned to lean against the bar and watch the crowd while sipping his ale, not noticing the hateful stare of his friend.

"Dern, it's busy tonight, ain't it?" Dusty said casually, looking around.

Carson did not reply. He kept glaring.

"I bet old Bernard is happy though," waving a hand behind him towards the bartender, who was also the owner of the Wary Sheep Saloon. He watched the table with Gente and Verrel for a moment, took a sip from his cup, and said, "Boy, she brings in a lot of business, doesn't she?"

"You would know," Carson growled, slamming his glass on the bar top.

The response surprised Dusty, who turned back to look at Carson and noticed his glare for the first time. "Huh? Something the matter, Beau?"

It was too late to dodge the fist when Dusty finally recognized one was coming. Carson's fist knocked the halfling off his stool and onto the ground.

"The hell is wrong with you, Beau?" Dusty shouted from the saloon floor. Carson stepped in to punch down at the ranger, forcing Dusty to roll backward over his shoulders and onto his feet. Carson stumbled and was wild-eyed, making fists at his sides.

"I saw you!" he yelled. "I saw you, you sneak. How much did you offer her? How dare you insult the lady and impugn her honor in front of me!" Carson shot a jab with his left hand, which Dusty ducked, but then followed it up with an uppercut with his right, which he did not dodge. It sent him back several steps, winded.

Dusty had no idea what had gotten into his friend. Trying to catch his breath, Dusty gasped, "Listen pard, I'm getting real sick of this . . . I don't know what you're talking about, but you need to calm down." The commotion had silenced the saloon and all eyes were on them as Carson continued to square off against the ranger.

"Don't you tell me to calm down, you mouse turd. She's mine!" Carson yelled and took swing after swing against the halfling, but he didn't get any more cheap shots now that Dusty was fully aware of the threat. Unimpaired by drink, Dusty's thinking was clearer and reflexes sharper than Carson's.

Carson never saw the quick, low jabs, but he felt them. Right, left, another left, then a strong right to the torso. Now he was the one doubled over, gasping for breath. But his anger wasn't spent yet. Carson stood, put his weight on his back foot, and rotated his hips away from Dusty before uncoiling a wild haymaker. Dusty side-stepped and Carson's weight continued through the punch into empty air. Dusty kicked out, tripping him and forcing him to fall to the saloon floor.

"I'm not going to fight you, Beau. This is stupid," Dusty said.

But Beau Carson was love drunk on a volatile cocktail of equal parts alcohol, jealousy, and false hopes. He stood and squared off against Dusty, then charged. Again Dusty sidestepped

the man, who plowed headfirst into a table occupied by card players. He lay still. Surprised at the
sudden end to the brawl, Dusty went to check on
him as the shire-reeve entered the Wary Sheep.

"Howdy, Orrin," Dusty said, looking up. He
nodded down at his unconscious friend. "I think
he hit his head and knocked himself out."

"What the hell started it, Dusty?" Shackleton
asked him.

"I'm not rightly sure. He seemed to think I had
made an . . . offer to the lady there," he said, gesturing at Verrel at a nearby table surrounded by
her admirers. "But I'd just walked in and ordered
a drink, then he started swinging."

The reeve nodded and then addressed the
crowded bar. "Alright folks, show's over! Back to
your drinks now. And keep it friendly!" He asked
Dusty to give him a hand with Beau. The tall
man dragged the cowhand out by his shoulders,
while the smaller halfling tried to carry him by
his boots. Some of the saloon patrons sniggered
before returning to their drinks or cards.

"You want him in the jail, Orrin?" Dusty asked the shire-reeve. "I don't think he was in his right mind and I won't be pressing charges."

"Yessir. Reckon he ought to sleep it off. I'll have Maybelle take a look at his head."

Together they hobbled down and across the street to the jail, got Carson through the door, and onto a cot in a cell. After locking the cell door, the reeve poured a cup of coffee in a tin cup from a pot that had been warming on a small stove and handed it to Dusty. He waved a hand at an empty chair across from a desk scattered with parchments, scrolls, and wanted posters. The halfling had been feeling lightheaded again, so he gladly took the seat and sipped the coffee.

They drank their coffee in silence for a while. The reeve took a deep breath and then blew it out slowly. "Dusty, it's been wild. Ever since those two got into town it's been madness every night."

Dusty chewed his lip. "I'm noticing it too. You know I caught Jed shirking his fire watch duty the other night? He was in the Wet Goat Saloon, acting a fool in front of the bar girls and caterwauling worse than a polecat."

"That's why you got him digging that well?"

Dusty nodded and sipped his coffee. Jed was a junior ranger in Dusty's troop. "And mucking the stables and all the KP. By himself." He took another sip. The coffee was helping him feel back to normal.

"It's that snake oil and that damn *girl*," Shackleton complained, turning in his seat to peer through the window at the Wary Sheep Saloon. "I can't prove it yet, though. With all the town losing their minds, I've been unable to properly investigate. I'm stretched thin, Dusty. Would you mind looking into it for me?"

Something pulled at Dusty, a whisper that seemed to get quieter the more coffee he had. He thought about it, and reluctantly agreed that Shackleton was right: this needed looking into. "I'll let you know what I find."

3

Dusty was in an alley between two stores across the street from the Wary Sheep and had a good view of the entrance and the street in both directions. He figured the two merchants would head back for their wagon and found an observation post in that direction. The night was dark, but he had retrieved his grey cloak from the barracks to break up his outline and help blend into the night.

He watched as people poured out of the swinging doors of the saloon and then broke off into little groups as they headed to their homes or one of the inns. Finally, he saw someone wearing a tall, feathered hat exit into the street, escorting a lady with her hand in his arm. That must be Gente. Verrel was wearing her hood again, hiding her face in the dark. They walked casually up the street, talking quietly while returning to camp. They had been offered free board at an inn, but they had graciously declined and pitched a large campaign tent near their wagon, with a canopy connecting the two structures to provide shade.

Dusty watched from the shadows, quiet and unmoving. After they walked past his position in the alley he slipped out and started tailing them, keeping cover behind water troughs, barrels, and wagons in the street. He made no sound, having made sure to leave his spurs off his boots and secured all jangling metal bits on his leather jerkin or belt. He carried a small dagger hanging from the left side of his belt and a tomahawk-shaped handaxe on his right. It was always better to have them and not need them than need them and not have them.

The two merchants approached their encampment on the outskirts of town, and Dusty watched them from the livery, peering over a corral that housed their donkeys as they entered their tent. He waited patiently in case one of them came out of the tent to attend to their animals or conduct some business at the garish wagon. After several minutes without seeing movement, he made his move.

But as soon as he began to break cover and sneak closer, the tent flap opened and the woman came out, carrying a bundle of something in her arms. In a flash, he ducked back behind the corral and rolled his eyes at the timing. He risked a glance and saw that she had paused outside for a moment. Dusty wasn't sure if she had seen him or not, but then she turned and walked towards a stream located outside of town.

As she got closer to the streambed the ground began sloping down. She found the path that the townsfolk had cut into the bank to have access to the water. It was a wide stream, which poured over a rock outcropping and formed a little pool before continuing south to the coast, giving Breckenridge Falls its name.

Dusty watched, crouched behind a boulder on the bank as Verrel came to the water's edge. She set her bundle down and opened it, setting aside a flask, a fleece, and a small rag, and then disrobed.

At that moment Dusty realized Verrel was going to take a bath and that he was peeping. As her robe came off he saw her slender body, supple and lithe like a willow. The moon was not bright, but he could still see, though not as much as he secretly wished. The woman took the flask and poured some of its contents onto the rag and then walked into the water up to her hips. She began to rub the rag on her body as she splashed water onto her arms and chest. She sang a soft, haunting melody while she bathed.

The temptation to watch was strong, but he forced himself to sit down behind the rock where he was hiding so that he was unable to see. Occasionally he peeked over the top to make sure she was still there, but he was disciplined not to let his eyes linger. He negotiated internally with himself. It didn't matter that he was a bachelor, it just wasn't right.

He seemed to have to tell himself that repeatedly as he sat there.

A few minutes went by, and he looked again. He saw that she had finished up with the rag and was swimming to rinse off. He sat back down, listening to the splashing and singing, and tried to figure out his next move. He wasn't sure what he was going to be able to accomplish with this reconnaissance other than feeling awkward. What he wanted to do was get a look inside the wagon or the tent, but that wouldn't be possible tonight. He would have to come again when Gente and Verrel were occupied in the town. Perhaps after one of their sales performances, or while they ate at the Falls Cafe. He kicked himself for not thinking about that earlier. Yet he stayed.

It had grown quiet, and Dusty realized he no longer heard the woman splashing or singing in the water. He risked a peep from around the rock. Verrel was gone, yet her bathing items were still there. A wet fleece had been draped over a fallen tree to dry.

"Damn fool," he muttered to himself and turned back. He saw then he was not alone.

There facing him stood Verrel, wearing her hooded robe. It was tied loosely but still clung tightly around her damp body in all the right places. She was looking at him, her face partially concealed, and he gaped up at her.

"I saw you watching," she said softly. Dusty didn't say anything in reply, partly from embarrassment, partly because he didn't know how to explain himself, and partly because of the beautiful near-naked woman standing in front of him.

"Does that happen a lot?" he finally asked.

"Sometimes," she said slowly and then took a step towards him. The moonlight revealed her eyes now, green slits in a pale face. "Something you wanted to see?" she asked teasingly in a sing-song voice.

Dusty stood and folded his cloak tight around him like a shield from her temptation. He had to find a way out of there. He no longer cared if it looked suspicious. He cleared his throat and then made to leave, but stopped, unable to take his eyes off of Verrel's. They were glinting in the night, transfixing him with her hungry gaze. Dusty had the impression of being a deer hunted by a catamount.

She stepped closer and was just in front of him. He could see her smiling now, an alluring smile, eyes locked on his. She gently took his hand and placed it on the belt of her robe. His fingertips grazed the bare flesh at her stomach where the robe was not tightly wrapped. "I bet there *is* something." When he didn't pull the belt on his own, she used his hand to pull it, untying the robe. It opened, revealing her smooth, hairless nudity underneath. Her beauty was a weapon, dangerous and coiled like a viper. He saw her impossibly long legs lead up into a strong torso with petite breasts suggestively covered by her long black hair.

Dusty wasn't even sure if he was awake anymore. "Ma'am . . ." he began to say. He was resisting heroically, but the pull remained. She cut him off by stepping into him and bending slightly, brushing him with her naked body. She looked into his eyes, paralyzing him. Then she kissed him.

She tasted like the elixir she hawked to the townsfolk, sweet with a hint of anise. She tasted like a warm summer night filled with forbidden acts. She tasted like exotic spices from faraway lands. It was a kiss that excited his passions. He wanted to dethrone kings and plunder their gold. He wanted to raid and rule. He wanted to jump off precipices and be caught by angels. He wanted to take her and devour her.

But then he tasted blood, and he grew lightheaded once more. She was no longer kissing him, but continued to smile, looking down at him, while he stepped backward and fell to the ground, dizzy. She had removed the hood from her head now, the robe still hanging from her shoulders framing her body. His eyes grew blurry and he couldn't see her. Something was wrong with her face. What was wrong with her face? He couldn't tell. And then he was asleep.

4

He was driftwood in a river. It was moving fast, bearing him along its current. He tried to move his arms to swim but he couldn't take them from his sides, nor could he kick his feet. He tried to call out but was choked by the water. Now he couldn't breathe. His brain started to panic as it fought to open his mouth for air. His lungs began to burn.

Dusty awoke lying on the ground and gasping for breath. He was face down in the dirt, and he coughed. He tried to sit up, but he couldn't move his limbs. He rolled onto his back, blinked a few times to adjust to the light, and worked to control his breathing.

He was in the campaign tent. His arms and legs were bound by rope. A small lantern sat on a crate in the corner, throwing a weak light into the canvased room. There were two cots with skins and fleeces, and a trunk sat along the wall of the tent. Underneath one of the cots was the biggest snake skin Dusty had ever seen on the frontier; longer than a rattler and many times its width. He shuddered as he stared at it, then forced himself to look away.

Dusty tested his bonds. The room felt muggy despite the semi-arid heat of Breckenridge Falls, and his arms were slick with sweat. He could wriggle his hands, but they were tied at the wrists behind his back, and his legs were tied at his ankles. He rolled his ankles and felt a familiar pressure on his right side. He smiled.

He shrimped and shimmied his way across the ground towards the trunk and threw his legs onto the lid. He began to saw his legs back and forth. He rubbed the rope on the edge of the trunk, using it to push against the coils. At last, he managed to push the rope up his legs and off his boots.

It was Dusty's habit to keep a folding knife in his right boot. He had been in tight spots before and no one ever seemed to check there. His dagger and axe had been taken, but they had not discovered his folder.

Lifting his legs, he jerked them in the air and felt the lump in his boot move. He jerked again and it moved some more. He jerked his legs a third time and it fell out and smacked his face.

Dusty breathed sharply and cursed. He wormed his body to the side until he felt the knife with his hands. He managed to open the blade and began sawing it across the hemp rope around his wrists. It was an odd angle and made for slow work—he sliced himself more than once—but he persisted and eventually cut his hands free.

He leaned over and cut the bonds around his legs. He stood, wiping blood from his wrists, and made a quick search of the room. He found his hat and put it on but didn't see his belt or weapons. He considered breaking the leg off a cot to act as a club, but he couldn't fathom how to do it without making noise.

He feared being caught by the two con artists so he limited his search. On a table was a small, black stone figure of a snake with a wide hood. Its eyes were encrusted by two small rubies. Next to the idol was a bowl of oblong eggs. They were longer than a chicken's and not as wide, but the shells felt soft and leathery, and Dusty began to feel a knot of dread deep in his gut.

He felt the cool night air blow in from a flap in the fabric and felt relief. He crept towards it, taking deliberate steps to maintain silence and stealth. He poked his head out the door and saw that he was in the merchants' tent. Before him was the sitting area under a canopy attached to the side of the large, brightly painted wagon. He could see light gleaming at him from a crack where the door was located in the wagon's side.

He crept out of the tent and past the canopy until he had his back against a wagon wheel. He looked underneath the wagon bottom, saw nothing, then looked around to each side. All he could see was the tent and the town in the distance. Did he make a run for it and alert the town? What would he even say, and would they believe him?

He slipped up to the door and peered through the crack, and then he wished he hadn't.

A lantern hung from the ceiling illuminating the inside of the wagon. Crates were piled at one end with bottles. Next to them, stood Gente, with his back to the door. "There," the man said. "That was a good batch. We need more though, mistress."

He heard Verrel's voice in reply, but it seemed slurred, and he couldn't hear the words. He kept watching, feeling like a peeping fool again, but this time he was the naked one without his weapons. Gente made little movements and then stepped away. He saw Verrel naked again, except instead of smooth skin, hers was loose and flaking, like flesh peeling from a bad sunburn. Were those . . . scales? Her skin rippled behind her ears and along her neck like a rash. Her eyes were slits, and her nose seemed flatter. Together with her red lips, it gave him the impression of a snake.

Gente returned with a glass carboy and handed it to Verrel, who, to Dusty's horror, opened her mouth and extended long, curved fangs. She hooked them against the lip of the carboy and a cloudy white liquid began to seep from the tips of the fangs and drop into the jar. She was milking.

Gente was over by the crates again, using a dropper to add the cloudy liquid milk from the carboy into bottles partially filled with a brown liquid. He stirred each one and then corked them. Gente walked to the other end to retrieve a stack of labels and the wagon moved, rocking the hanging lantern above.

"Careful, fool!" Verrel hissed through her fangs. "You know how flammable thiss is."

Gente gave an annoyed grunt in reply but carefully walked back to the other side to continue bottling the elixir.

"What did you do with the halfling?" she asked.

"He is tied in our chambers, mistress. I think he would make a good sacrifice to Seth before we take the town," he replied.

"Good." She drew out the word. "It wass difficult to hold him in the charm. He resissted sstrongly," Verrel said. She stood, handing the carboy to Gente. Then she took a slender hand and started to peel away the loose skin from her shoulders. It fell off her in great flakes, covering the wagon floor. Each peeled layer revealed scales, like freckles. "Our plan is working. If we can remove the other rangerss, then it will be easier for us when our people come to this land. Thiss town is already ourss! No one can ressisst uss now."

That was all he needed to know. Dusty crept back to the tent where he had been bound, retrieved the lantern, and then snuck back to the wagon, shielding the light of the little flame with his hat. His face was grim and determined. With one smooth action, he snapped open the door and smashed the lantern against a crate of elixir. He slammed the door shut and barred it with a board across its latches.

The two merchants were trapped inside and screaming. It was a horrid, hissing scream that could be heard from the town and woke mothers and children. They tried to beat against the door, but the flames had caught too quickly and in no time the entire wagon was an inferno of flame. Dusty had to step away from the heat. He found a lounge chair under the canopy and sat, watching it burn.

Green flames roared into the night. After the screams died, Dusty made a more thorough search of the tent. Inside, he found a book of parchments wrapped in leather. It contained a detailed ledger recording shipments into Sumadea and some letters.

The town was eventually roused by the flames and came running to the encampment. They found the engulfed ruin of the wagon and Dusty reading the documents in a chair. Later, he made a report to the shire-reeve and explained what he had found. Shackleton looked alarmed at Dusty's description of Verrel's asp-like fangs and the milking process as the source of the "miracle elixir." He wasn't delighted that Dusty had burned the wagon down, but he wasn't in the mood to fuss over it either.

In the morning Dusty was back in town at the Falls Cafe helping Freddy Gaines, the chief waitress, brew pots and pots of coffee. It seemed the whole town was hungover after waking up from a charmed but restless sleep. Any man or woman who had purchased and consumed the elixir now faced fierce headaches and nausea. Dusty and Freddy distributed the coffee to the townsfolk gathered in groups outside the cafe.

As he handed a cup of coffee to Jed, the junior ranger who had skipped out on his fire watch, a group of four riders came galloping into town. Something seemed familiar about them, but it wasn't until they dismounted their horses that Dusty placed them. They were the riders he had chased away from the wagon, three men and a half-elf.

They tied off their mounts and then made their way through the crowd. One spotted Dusty and called out to the others. They looked up and found him leaning against the threshold of the restaurant, watching them. They headed straight for him.

"Howdy," Dusty said. He had handed a cup to a man sitting on nearby steps and then turned to face the four with his hands tucked into his belt.

"Are you Lieutenant Dusty Thorngage?" one of the men asked.

"Yes."

"You're under arrest for interfering with an imperial investigation," the man said.

Dusty stared at them, without blinking. "Say that again."

The man frowned and repeated. "I said, you're under arrest. We are with the Sumadean Customs Bureau. We were tracking two con artists, a man and a mongrel woman."

"What do you mean by mongrel?" The shire-reeve stepped up next to Dusty and eyed the others with suspicion. There were all kinds of "half-breeds" in Breckenridge Falls, from half-orcs to half-elves.

"Her kind are demon worshippers from far away. Part snake and part human. They sacrifice people to some being they call Set, or sometimes Seth. We were in pursuit of them four days ago when you interfered and assaulted us."

Dusty laughed. "Assault? I never touched you, just your bridle. My pony bit the pile of soap bones you were riding; you going to arrest him for assault?"

"This is no laughing matter, Lieutenant," one of the men said.

"Oh yes it is," Dusty retorted.

The first man was unsmiling. They had been reprimanded when their superiors learned the patrol had been routed by a single halfling. He was angry with the shame of it. "Stop your talk and let's go. I'm taking you in."

It grew quiet and all eyes were on the four larger folk standing off against the halfling. Then at once every townsperson in the streets and on the sidewalk, everyone who had a table at the cafe, and everyone in the neighboring buildings stood up or came outside. They were glaring, and some were brandishing weapons. Beau Carson came to stand next to Dusty.

"No. You're not," Dusty said.

"No? You let the fugitives get away!" The man from the customs bureau demanded.

"No he didn't," Carson replied, staring hard at the four.

"Then where are they?" the man asked, holding his hands out as if looking for them.

"Burned them," Dusty replied simply. He tossed them the leather book with the letters and records and walked into the cafe for another round of coffee.

SPIRIT OF THE DESERT
By: Curtis Moore

Mark was careful about calling unlikely-sounding animals "mythical." As a gnome who rode an armored fighting chicken, he'd been labeled mythical more than once, and explaining that he was real to people was exhausting. Besides, it didn't have the same ring as "legendary," or even the same scholarly bent as "folkloric." It was dismissive. But when he saw a rabbit with shining silver antlers moving through the low desert brush, he didn't have another word for it. He touched the crossbow that hung from his saddle and reined in Wildfire, his battle chicken, and followed the creature into the brush.

This was not, strictly speaking, a part of his mission. Wrenda, the dwarf priestess who had some kind of interdimensional seeing ability she would never fully explain to him, sent him here to find a spirit causing trouble in the desert and report back to her. It was a quick trip for him, using the gnome tunnels that most of his kin used to steal goods from one world and sell them at exorbitant prices in other worlds where they were rare. Instead of bags of roasted coffee beans, he was stealing information.

"It's a being of air and fire without a body," she had explained to him, as if that was any explanation at all. "And it's killing people."

"And you want me to visit violence upon it? Bring an end to its reign of terror?"

Wrenda shook her head, her dark eyes narrowed. "This isn't like killing that were-skunk in Avekko. These spirits are dangerous."

"Were-skunks are dangerous."

"They can," Wrenda went on, "wreak extraordinary damage in the space of just a few moments. They can possess bodies if they find a willing vessel. They will lie their way in, promis-

ing all sorts of favors and aid to the unsuspecting. Their only goal is to spread destruction. You
need to be careful."

Careful. People loved telling Mark to be careful.
He only came up to Wrenda's chest, and she was
on the short side even for the dwarves whose re-
ligion she administered. On the surface, among
the big people, he only came up to most folks'
knees. Every time someone almost stepped on
him they would say something like, "Ope, almost
got ya there. Be careful."

Mark sniffed at the memory, even as a tumble-
weed twice his size rolled past him, and turned
back to the task at hand. The antlered rabbit
might be a clue, or it might be the thing itself. He
wound through the sagebrush forest, following
the animal's bounding tracks. The thing could
have left Mark miles behind in no time. Unaware
of him, it instead meandered through clearings,
stopping to nibble tender new brush growth or
to scrape its bright antlers against the trunks of
bushes. Mark rolled a length of rope between his
fingers; if he could just get close enough . . . His
heart leapt at the idea.

Mark—and other security gnomes—tended to ride chickens, particularly roosters. Their natural aggression was easy to channel, and they were agile in combat. The old gnomes used to ride rabbits on the surface because of how far and fast they could travel. Mark could already travel vast distances with the gnomes' tunnels, so he had never been interested in any mount just for their speed or endurance. Never, at least, until now.

His confidence solidified: the horned rabbit was corporeal. Wrenda hadn't mentioned anything, but he had never heard of a desert spirit who nibbled on sagebrush or left little pellets in their wake. That would be extraordinary attention to detail to throw off a gnome who had only been on this plane of existence for an hour.

He was so focused on the rabbit's tracks he almost missed seeing it charge him. Wildfire was alert though, and the big chicken spun away just in time for the hooked horns to pass by them. Nearly unseated in the whirl, Mark barely pushed his foot back into his stirrup when the rabbit spun around and charged again. With his weapons tied down for traveling, Mark deployed his most effective escape measure. With a shrill whistle, he leapt Wildfire—wings beating—over a nearby cholla. The rooster landed some fifty feet away in a dead run. The thump of the rabbit's feet closed on them. Mark's fingers settled on the quick-release knots that held his crossbow in place. He was going to have to take more extreme measures if his situation didn't improve a whole lot in a short time.

They sped across the base of a granite out-cropping. Spotting a faint trail take off up the hill, he took it on an impulse. Twisting in his seat, his eyes met the creature's beady red ones as it emerged from the brush and gathered itself for another charge. This time there was nothing for them to escape behind. He flipped down his eyepatch so he could aim better and jerked the knot holding his crossbow.

His head smashed into something soft and wooly, and there was a bleat of surprise as two cloven hooves barely missed his head. Mark kept his seat and reeled in the saddle as he looked for this latest threat. It was a sheep. Rather, there were several sheep looking dumbly at him, and one sheep that was bouncing down the hill away from him. The sudden clatter of the gravel was loud in the wash.

A small part of his mind puzzled over the sheep. It was an unlikely place for them, unless there was a herder nearby. But a herder should have at least shouted some obscenities at him for ramming one of his sheep off a cliff. There was no sign of people anywhere. Although, this part of the trail was suspiciously well maintained.

The trail made an abrupt climb up the rocky outcropping, then bent suddenly into a pocket. A man was standing there, holding a huge hammer in one hand and an iron stake in the other.

"Run!" Mark almost always had to shout to make sure humans heard him, and it helped to keep his words short and the ideas simple.

The man seemed unable to move. When Mark was just a few feet away, he bolted toward the cliff face. Wildfire knew his business and matched the man stride for stride. Mark held his crossbow ready, his head swiveling between the man and the trail where the creature would appear. He thought he saw the flash of silver antlers when suddenly the ground angled sharply down. Metal and wood clanged, and the man swore as he tripped over something, then ran on. Darkness swept over Mark, and the air turned cool. The smell of settled earth washed over him, and he breathed a sigh. They were in a tunnel.

Now they were on Mark's ground. No human could match a gnome underground. His eyes adjusted rapidly, showing the man standing in the corner with a pickaxe over his shoulder. Mark vaulted from the saddle and took cover behind a timber.

"Explain yourself, now," he demanded. "Is that thing your familiar, or are you bound to it?"

The man didn't lower the pickaxe, but he did take a deep breath in. "What?"

"That thing with the antlers. Is it yours, or do you belong to it?"

"You saw it too?"

"Was hard not to. If I hadn't been well-mounted it would have gored me straight through." He dug a mealworm from his pouch and tossed it to the chicken. "Good boy, Wildfire."

"I knew it was real." This time the man did lower the pickaxe and take a step toward where Mark stood. "But anyone I told said that jackalopes were mythical."

"People are reckless with that word." Mark turned back toward the mouth of the tunnel. There was no sign of the jackalope. "What are you doing out here?"

"I'm prospecting, right now." The man gestured with the pickaxe as if that would prove his vocation. "But I have other jobs."

Mark lowered his crossbow and flipped up his eyepatch so he could really regard the man and the tunnel. He was young, slightly built, wearing a plaid shirt and patched jeans that were no color in particular. His knees were skinned from tripping as he ran earlier. Mark looked toward the entrance and saw a pile of tools scattered from being kicked.

"Did you just have that eyepatch on to look cool?"

"It helps me aim. What's a jackalope?"

The man shrugged. "Beats me. The only one I've seen before this is hanging up as a joke in a bar a hundred miles from here."

"But you've seen this one now?"

"I thought I was losing it. I guess I still might be. I never thought that . . . well, what are you?"

"A gnome."

"Right. I never thought gnomes existed, or giant chickens. Those seem mythical to me. So, it's possible you all exist or that I'm in worse trouble than I imagined."

"There's that word again. But, yes, we exist. My name is Mark, if that makes it easier."

"Honestly it just raises more questions. My name is Artzai, though."

"Is that a common name here?"

"Not in this country."

Wildfire rested his head against Mark's shoulder, and he stroked the hard beak while he thought. If he tried to catch up to the jackalope again it might just anger it more. He needed to find a place to camp and then reassess in the morning. His real mission was the desert spirit anyway; he had no business with jackalopes.

"I need to clean up and get back to my wagon," Artzai said. "It's not far from here, if you want to join me."

Mark's eyes narrowed. Why would a person he had just met, who apparently didn't believe in gnomes, invite him to his wagon for dinner? It was suspicious. He ran a finger along his belt and palmed a coin Wrenda had made for just this purpose. It was pure silver and had her name along with a bunch of runes he couldn't read along the edge.

"There it is again!" He pointed behind the man.

Artzai turned to look, and Mark stepped forward and threw the coin at the back of his head. It bounced off his thick black hair and fell heavily to the ground.

"Ouch." Artzai knelt and picked up the coin. "Why did you do that?"

Mark eyed the man's fingers, trying to remember everything Wrenda had told him. "You don't manipulate air or fire, do you?" He walked over and snatched the coin. "I'm supposed to find a desert spirit out here, and you were acting suspicious. It was a precaution."

"Suspicious? I invited you to my wagon for dinner, and to stay if you wanted to."

"Exactly. Who does that? Especially if they don't believe in gnomes."

"Well, I believe in them now. I'd be crazy not to, wouldn't I?"

"Do you believe in jackalopes?"

"I guess I have to."

"Do you have to see something to believe in it?"

Artzai shrugged. "You've got me there. I believed there was silver in that hole before I saw any of it."

Mark followed his gesture down the narrow tunnel gouged into the rock, supported by dark timbers.

"Is that what you're prospecting for?"

"I'm not picky. But it's what that hole is for."

"Is there any silver in it?"

Artzai leaned down and picked a rock up from a pile. It glittered in the sun as he held it out to Mark. "There's high-grade ore in there."

Mark studied the rock, turning it in his fingers before handing it back. "It looks like something's been chewing on it."

Artzai shrugged. "Rocks break in weird ways."

A sheep bleated in the distance, and Artzai tilted his head, listening. When he moved again, he walked to the pile of tools and started to put them in some kind of order. "I have to get back for dinner and get the flock to bed."

Mark followed him, eyeing the rotten timbers near the entrance suspiciously. "I thought you were a prospector."

Artzai didn't say anything until he finished stacking a shovel, pickaxe, and hatchet against the wall of the tunnel. "I'm a prospector right now. In a minute I'll be a shepherd. Then I'll be a cook. Then a tinsmith when I fix the flue on my stove."

"Must be hard to get help if you've got four jobs."

Artzai jerked his shoulder a little, then said, "I'll have help soon. I'm learning how to find it. I'm reading a book on it."

Mark nodded. Wrenda had insisted he read some leadership books as well.

"Are you an odd sort of fellow on this side?" Mark asked.

"This side of what?" Artzai pointed toward some low mountains in the distance. "The mountains? There aren't many people over here to compare to, so I might be."

"I'll take that as a yes."

Artzai gave him a lopsided smile and turned to walk back up the draw. "Not nearly as odd as someone who rides a chicken and chases jackalopes."

As they walked, sheep appeared out of the brush. Some turned quietly up the draw with no encouragement, others required a small "hup" or a clicking noise from Artzai before they started moving. They seemed to know where they were going, and before long they made a loose circle around a green wagon that was roofed with tin.

Odd or not, Artzai was a good cook. He waved away Mark's offer of dried beef and beans and pulled a cast iron oven out of a hole lined with smoldering coals. The steam that billowed from it when he took the lid off carried the mingling scents of tomatoes, peppers, garlic, and maybe white wine. The rush of the chase was gone, and now hunger washed over Mark. His mouth watered, and when Artzai dropped a thick slice of crusty bread into a coffee cup and handed it to him he thought it might be worth burning his tongue on it just to try a bite of it sooner. Instead, he held the cup on his knees and watched as the shepherd spooned himself a helping in a shallow ceramic bowl.

"What is this?"

"Sukalki," Artzai said simply.

It was a good enough explanation, so Mark blew on his stew, sopped up some broth with his bread, and took a bite. It was just as good as it smelled, and they ate in silence.

Artzai finished his stew and rose and walked among the sheep, muttering to himself and flipping through a small, black leather book. Mark didn't watch him work because it seemed rude. He tended to Wildfire, checked his weapons, and rolled out his bedroll in a sandy spot beneath Artzai's wagon. When the shepherd returned, they had a short, polite argument regarding who should sleep in the wagon and who should sleep outside, but in the end the sleeping arrangements remained the same, and they went to bed. Mark covered himself with his blankets and rolled over.

From under the wagon he could hear Artzai's voice, then the loud turning of a page, then more reading. It was in a language Mark didn't understand, but there were a lot of languages he didn't understand. He closed his eyes. There was a sudden thump from inside the wagon that made him jump. He started to rise, then remembered Artzai was going to fix his chimney and went back to sleep.

The desert morning brought a coolness that surprised Mark. Moisture clung to the ends of his dark red beard and settled over his blankets in millions of droplets that reflected the sky's growing gray light. Toads chirped somewhere close by. He sat for a moment, feeling the peace of the morning spread through him. Did the other gnomes, the ones who didn't get involved with surface problems or dwarf priestesses, have time to enjoy mornings like this?

It was too much thinking this early in the morning. He rose, belted on his sword, his knife, his backup knife, his ankle knife, his backup ankle knife, and rolled his blankets together. His movements were practiced but unhurried. By the time he had saddled Wildfire and breathed life into the banked coals the sun was a thin line against the horizon. He wrestled Artzai's huge percolating pot onto the fire and filled it with coffee and sat with his own small cup, enjoying the quiet bubbling sound the blue pitcher made.

He didn't know what time the . . . tinsmith? Prospector? Shepherd. His main job seemed to be connected to the sheep. He had a notebook for them, after all. He didn't know what time the shepherd would wake up, but the sheep seemed somewhat put out. They bleated and stomped. Mark had very limited contact with surface livestock, but he was pretty sure they didn't usually make this much noise. Twice he considered knocking on the wagon door, but both times he stopped himself. It wasn't any of his business how Artzai did his job. The sheep weren't locked up or anything. They must just be waiting for Artzai to push them back down the draw. It was about time for him to leave, anyway.

He bridled his chicken and looked at the campsite. He should leave a note. Artzai had a book, so he could read, but were his alphabet and Mark's the same? Maybe he should just draw a smiley face in the sand. He picked up a stick to do just that when he heard the wagon open.

"Morning," he said as Artzai stepped down.

The sound startled the shepherd, and he tripped headlong coming out the door. He made no attempt to stop his fall, and he landed on the hard ground with an unsettling crunch.

Mark dropped Wildfire's reins and ran to the man. Artzai's eyes were open, darting around, but his expression remained neutral.

"A slip." Artzai spoke as if he wasn't laying face-down in the dirt. "They happen sometimes before . . ." His voice went oddly flat for a moment. "Before I've had my coffee."

Mark frowned, looking at Artzai's neck and head for some sign of whatever had crunched.

His mouth worked, and even now his hands and legs were starting to move, even if the movements were slow. Maybe the crunch had just been the gravel?

Mark stepped back and let the man put one hand under himself and push up, then coil his legs until he was in a kneeling position. He sat there for a moment, his eyes wide to the sky like a supplicant without a specific god to pray to, then lurched to his feet.

Mark dragged a cup of coffee toward him. He had seen people who needed their coffee, but Artzai had to be a special case if he lacked all motor control before he got it.

"Thank you, gnome," Artzai said as he drank.

"It's Mark," he corrected him, and he walked to where Wildfire stood. "Unless you just want me to call you 'shepherd,' or 'tinsmith', or whatever."

Artzai made no move, still holding the cup to his mouth. "We won't see each other again, so names aren't necessary now. You were going?"

It was hard to square the generous, smiling shepherd/prospector/cook from the night before with the person talking to him now. It didn't matter to Mark, though. If that's how people in this world were, then he didn't plan on spending any more time in it than he had to. Shoot, if that's how they were all the time, no wonder even their cute animals had to grow horns.

"I'll find that desert spirit and then get out of here as fast as I can." He brought a foot up to his stirrup, then stopped. Artzai's head had turned, too far around to be comfortable, or even natural, to stare at him. His eyes were still wide, but his face now projected a malevolence that was impossible to miss.

"You don't need"—Artzai lurched upright and paused, swaying on his feet. His voice was cold, and his jaw made no attempt to move as he spoke—"to look any further, little gnome. Why do you seek me?"

Mark palmed the silver coin and swung into the saddle. "I was only sent to find you. I'm not interested in anything you're selling."

Artzai's body made a sudden lunge toward him, but the knees buckled halfway through his step, and he slammed into the ground again. Mark hurled the coin at him. The silver made a hissing sound as it burned into flesh. Wildfire wheeled and bolted for the arroyo he'd crossed into the day before.

Mark kept his head low as Wildfire sped through the brush. He could come back for the jackalope some other time. Right now, he needed to get out of here and report to . . .

"Wrenda?" A voice came from above. Now, not maintaining any pretense of humanity, it was just using Artzai's body to fly low above the desert floor. "I can't let you make it back to her, little gnome. This isn't personal."

He said that, but the burst of magic that incinerated a short pinyon tree in front of Mark seemed very personal. Wildfire jumped to the right to avoid another blast that dislodged a boulder, then to the left just in time to make Artzai's hammer miss. He didn't move fast enough to prevent a spinning, glowing, and clearly enchanted horned toad from smacking Mark right in his helmet.

He hit the ground hard on his back. His eyes spun. All he could see was blue sky, tan ground. Wildfire stopped, and he knew the chicken would come back and defend him to the death if he had to.

"Away, Wildfire!" he tried to shout, but his lungs were heaving and he couldn't get any air. Still, he heard the smallest of echoes, and he hoped he was loud enough. He drew his sword and pulled himself to his feet using a bush with a yellow flower on it.

"It isn't personal," the spirit said again from somewhere behind him, and Mark turned. "It's just that if Wrenda knows where I am, she'll come to stop me. And while shepherds who dabble in sorcery and overconfident gnomes are no problem for me, I fear she would prove more of a challenge."

Mark shook his head and tried to blink the dust out of his eyes. He could see a dark space to his side, but he could also see a figure floating upright with his hands held before him as if in benediction. Energy crackled between them, and he knew that at any moment it would flash toward him and end him here.

He blinked again and looked at a small, ragged hole to his right. Nothing good lived in holes like that, but whatever was in there was certainly better than what was out here. He rolled toward it, and his armor was suddenly hot as the magic bolt exploded and threw him forward into the darkness.

Something rustled. Just a few minutes ago, before he'd been chased underground by a body-possessing spirit, Mark would have said underground rustling was his least favorite sound. True, gnomes lived underground. But gnomic tunnels were usually well-lit. Even digging teams had piles of torches or battery-powered lights they stole from other worlds. He had one of those lights in his bedroll, tied right behind Wildfire's saddle and nowhere near enough to be useful. Hopefully the chicken was somewhere hiding now.

A shadow slid over the edge of the tunnel, and Artzai's panicking eyes showed along with the strangely calm face.

"This isn't fair. The earth dampens all my magic. Come out here where we can be on even ground."

Mark didn't reply. He had no illusions of fair play where this thing was concerned.

"Don't make me come in there," the spirit's voice was suddenly harsh. "Bodies don't come along every day, you know, and I don't want to waste this one chasing you."

Mark didn't speak. Unappealing as it was, he would take his chance with the rustling something. He turned into the darkness and extended a hand.

Both he and the rustle-maker jumped as his hand touched something excessively soft. He had expected something scaly with fangs and probably some kind of stinger. Instead, he got softness. His hand moved to the side and, well, there it was. There was a horn. He didn't even have to guess what this thing was. He had seen its blazing red eyes just the day before, and he couldn't imagine the jackalope was any happier to see him this time, now that there was a murdering, slightly self-absorbed spirit on his tail.

The jackalope did not charge. Instead, it stepped past Mark. Rather, since the quarters were so tight, it shoved Mark aside and started to squeeze past him. A most un-rabbitish noise rumbled from deep within its chest. Pressed against the animal's rib cage as he was, the sound reverberated through his own body, filling him at once with fear and elation. What was this thing? What could it do? Was this the bravado of a cornered animal, or did it have some power to resist the spirit?

"If you have gas," the spirit said, "good manners would dictate you pass it outside, rather than inside the burrow of whatever creature you're bothering. If you come out now, I'll give you a moment to release it. I wouldn't want to eat a gassy gnome anyway. It causes bloating, you know."

The jackalope shook its head and shifted, and Mark felt some relief, followed by a swell of despair. He was going to die here. The jackalope might turn on him and kill him in this burrow, or the spirit would leave Artzai's body and come in to kill him. Either way, he was done. He allowed himself a moment of self-pity. There was so much he had wanted to do before, well, before this. He would never get to sail on a ship, write his memoirs, or joust against the rats in the Riverton sewer. All those chances, gone. Just the day before he had wanted to ride this jackalope. No chance of that now.

The thought struck him, and he smiled to himself so suddenly it hurt his cheek. He could still ride the jackalope. It might—it would, probably—be the last thing he did. But he could do it. He reached out and ran his fingers through the thick hair. It would give him a decent handhold. He just needed to get up behind the shoulder and take his chance. The tunnel was high enough to accommodate its horns, so Mark could just fit if he leaned as close to the animal's neck as possible.

Without pausing to think too long about it, he vaulted onto the jackalope's back. The physical strength of the creature was shocking as it bunched its muscles and bounded forward. Mark buried his face in its fur, keenly aware of the rocky ground all around him. The spirit jerked away from the silver horns. Its body landed with a thud—it was still struggling to control Artzai's body when it wasn't flying—and then they were speeding down the arroyo.

He lifted his head slightly, and the wind lifted his beard behind him in a crimson trail. Familiar landmarks from the day before dimly registered as the jackalope tore past them at a speed Mark hadn't thought was even possible.

A blast of magic sent sand into his eyes, and Mark cursed. When he blinked the sand out and looked up, he recognized where they were, and his heart jumped. This was the trail that led to Artzai's mine. The jackalope knew it, and suddenly the chewing marks on the rocks made sense.

They tore along the mountainside, and he chanced a glance backward. The spirit was flying low over the brush, its face split in a wider grin than Artzai ever could have managed. Mark put his heels to the jackalope's sides, and it picked up speed, jumping over the tools near the entrance and bolting into the hole.

Gnomes' eyes adjust quickly, but even so there was a moment where the complete darkness enveloped him. The jackalope stopped and turned back to face the entrance to the mine. He remembered the glittering, high-grade ore Artzai had shown him the day before. There was no chance the spirit was coming in here.

A shadow fell across the wall as a foot crunched on gravel, and Mark cursed out loud. He deserved this for positive thinking.

"I find it amusing," the spirit said quietly into the dark, "that just an hour ago this place would have been entirely off-limits to me. This much exposed silver would have burned me to a crisp. But now," he reached out and stroked the walls of the mine with a finger, "I could spend the day in here if I packed a lunch."

The jackalope slunk across the wall toward the back of the mine, taking refuge behind a rotting timber. It had chased Mark with no hesitation the day before, but there was a size difference here. And, if it had any sense of self-preservation, it could probably sense the aura of malevolent magic that radiated off of Artzai now. Mark could. Or else Artzai was starting to rot already. Either way, it wasn't pleasant to be around.

"Speaking of, I can see you. I hate to spend my first hours in this generously donated meat suit in such an undignified chase. I have places to be and entire peoples to destroy. Wrenda would try to stop all that, and so I need you gone. By the time you're missed, I will have a comfortable head start, and she'll probably forget about me for another hundred years or so. Forgetful thing, isn't she?"

The spirit's spell was working on Mark. Something in the lilt of its voice and the rhythm of its words closed his mind to the danger he was in.

Its hand shot toward him. The jackalope jumped back, nearly throwing Mark off, and bolted further into the tunnel.

The spirit cursed and sent a bolt of magical fire at Mark, but the silver in the mine absorbed the spell before it could travel more than a few inches. He urged the jackalope on.

The roof was lower here. If Mark had dared stand on the jackalope's back he could almost have reached the top. Obviously he couldn't, even without the threat of a murderous spirit behind him. He and the jackalope were definitely aligned in their interest in staying away from this thing. If they were away from it and out in the open, he wasn't sure how it would feel about him. For Mark's part, he loved the feel of it. Its every move was grace itself. It was like riding a cloud on a windy day. Like riding a leaf down a rushing stream.

"It occurs to me you don't understand your position, gnome." The spirit was bent low but moving at speed through the tunnel. "I am offering to kill you. The alternative is for me to eat you and consume your soul. To add you to the maelstrom that sustains me so you can experience this, forever. Let me kill you."

That was reasonable.

The jackalope started back down the tunnel. It was growing darker the farther they wound into the mountainside. Mark's eyes could barely pick out the walls here, and it was getting so narrow he could almost touch both sides with his outstretched hands.

A sudden curse from behind made him flinch. Even knowing it couldn't use magic, there was no telling what the spirit would try next. Mark could barely make out the shape of Artzai's body kneeling in the passage, shaking his finger in front of him.

"This skin is so thin! Why should it tear so easily? It burns, gnome. I will set this against your account when I come to settle with you."

"You'd better work on your multiplication tables, then," Mark shouted down the tunnel, then cringed. That hadn't been his best work.

His head touched the roof of the tunnel and Mark's heart sank. This would be the end, then. Artzai couldn't have gotten this far in. Chances were the vein was in a natural fissure, and Artzai was just following it. The jackalope stopped, and Mark stepped off.

"Thanks for getting me this far." He rubbed the thick fur along the animal's shoulders. "I hope you can get out."

It turned toward him, and its silver antlers caught the tiny traces of light that made their way into the tunnel. Mark ran a finger along one and scratched the base of the horn.

"I wish we'd had more time together."

"Wishes are like fishes, you can catch them in your hand," the spirit sang softly as it approached. "Wishes are like fishes, and they'll die here in the sand."

Mark drew his sword. It was plain, honest steel. Nothing that would harm a spirit. It was all he had, and it was what he would use. The jackalope pressed against him, like it was offering or taking some reassurance from the contact. Mark tightened his grip on the sword and stepped forward. He wasn't going to die huddled in the back of this tunnel like a scared rabbit, present company excluded. He looked at the approaching figure and took in a deep breath.

"I don't know how old you are, spirit, but that meter and rhyme scheme is the most basic trash I've ever heard."

The spirit's eyes flamed in the darkness. "I didn't realize I was dealing with such a renowned scholar. Tell me, gnome, what would you have preferred?"

"At least a sonnet. Maybe a limerick, if you're feeling cheeky."

"I will try harder in future. We're going to be so close. Soon, we'll have time to work on..."

The hand shot out again, but Mark was ready this time. He plunged his blade into Artzai's forearm. Hot blood scalded his hands, and he let go and staggered back. The blood sizzled as it touched the silver-rich ground, and the smell of it made him nauseous.

The spirit didn't stop to speak. It was done taunting, ready to end this game. It wrenched the sword from its forearm, muttering curses in a dozen different languages, and lurched forward. Mark could hear and smell more of the burning blood as it slunk through the darkness. His sword edge glittered in the dim light as he took another step back. Something rolled under his foot, and he fell backward, landing hard on something sharp.

He cursed and reached down to grab whatever he'd fallen on. It was hard, round, and the light from the spirit's flaming eyes caught its graceful curves and points. It was one of the jackalope's shed antlers, and it was pure silver. The crafty thing chewed silver to grow those horns and then shed them again down here. He felt the horned rabbit's cold nose press against his hand. No wonder it had known these tunnels so well.

If the spirit noticed Mark's new weapon at all it didn't check its speed even a little. It advanced, holding Mark's sword high. Mark rocked on his feet, trying to find the exact right timing. The sword arced down toward him, and Mark stepped in and drove the point of the antler hard toward Artzai's armpit.

The sword cut a line of white heat down his back, and the boiling ichor of the spirit burned his face. But the spirit was screaming and thrashing now, and he saw his chance. He swung aboard the jackalope, and it leapt over Artzai's body and then they were sprinting down the tunnel.

It was too bad about Artzai. He deserved better than this. He'd been generous, and judging from the depth of this tunnel, hard-working. Mark pulled up, unsure of whether the jackalope would respond. It did, and together they looked back down the tunnel. Mark immediately wished they hadn't.

Artzai was elongating. His arms and legs were merging with his extending body. Soon Artzai's original form was lost, except for two long wounds and his shock of black hair. Smoke erupted from every place it touched the ground, and soon all he could see were its glowing eyes.

The jackalope spun and ran toward the entrance. Mark wanted nothing more than to be out of the mine, but he also knew that once they were out of the mine the spirit would have no limitations.

The light was better closer to the entrance. They tore past the stacked tools, past the dun lanterns, past the rotting timbers. The timbers!

Mark jumped off the jackalope and hit the ground. That hurt. Everything hurt. But he could see the tools right in front of him, all too big for him to use. All, except the hatchet.

Smoke billowed out of the tunnel now. He could barely make out two pinpricks of flame in the depth of the tunnel. Someone was screaming. Was it him, or whatever was left of Artzai?

Chips flew from the timber as he slammed the hatchet into it. Mark worked with a fury that made the wound on his back pour blood, made his muscles burn, and sent bolts of pain through his arms with every stroke. The eyes were getting closer. The smell was getting stronger. The timber groaned and cracked. Dust fell from the roof, then larger rocks. The earth above shuddered, and Mark turned and ran for the light. Something hit his foot, and he stumbled, tumbled, scrambled to his feet, then stood and ran again.

Mark didn't take his first real, full breath until he got his beard tangled in a cholla he tried to crawl over. He listened, and all he heard around him was silence. Pure, blessed silence. His fingers worked quickly, removing himself from the thorns. When he was free, he sat down and took another deep breath.

The crunch of gravel brought him immediately to his feet. He spun around, unsure whether running again would even be worth it. If the spirit wanted to kill him this bad, well, maybe it deserved to.

The regal figure of Wildfire, his jet-black battle chicken, materialized from the brush. The rooster strutted forward, feathers ruffled as he peered behind him, searching for the last threat he had seen. Mark threw his arms around the chicken and wept, telling him in short bursts everything that had happened. Wildfire's head rested on his shoulder, and for a moment they were still.

It was the flash of silver that got his attention. Mark opened his eyes fully, surprised to see the jackalope standing just a few feet away. Wildfire cocked his head, then nosed at Mark's pocket for a mealworm. Mark dropped one on the ground and held a hand toward the furry head. The jackalope stepped forward and met him.

"Are you coming back with me?" he asked.

The jackalope pressed harder against his hand.

"Okay." He reached behind Wildfire's saddle and took down a short length of rope that he fashioned into a halter. Tying it to another piece of rope, he took the lead and stepped into Wildfire's saddle. "Let's go home."

MIRACLE AT BISHOP'S BLUFF

BY: MICHAEL JOHN PETTY

It was mid-afternoon when Shane Cassidy arrived at Bishop's Bluff, and he was dead tired. It had been a grueling journey from the desert hellscape he'd left behind in Arizona, and he was thrilled to find refuge among the snowcapped mountains. The peaks glistened like angels in the cloudless sky, though the gunslinger's Stetson kept his eyes from enrapturement.

He had approached the settlement at the right time, as his horse—a prized Thoroughbred he'd picked up down south—showed signs of fatigue and needed the rest.

Shane could relate.

The town wasn't much to look at. A single, muddy strip ran up along a frosted hillside, banked by a thick array of lodgepole pines, which offered a dash of privacy to this remote outpost. Riding into town, Shane passed a newly built church house, clad in white and armed with a belled steeple that likely rang at the top of every hour.

Main Street had all the usual trappings the gunslinger had come to expect from these sorts of settlements. The Baker Hotel was the first to greet him with its wide front porch and decadent green trim around each window. Across the way sat the mercantile, and right beside that the Silver Spur Saloon. There was a bank as well, tucked two doors down from the hotel, and a sheriff's office just beside that, though it appeared to be vacant.

Satisfied with the accommodations, the wanderer deemed this spot as good as any to cease his wandering. At least for now.

Before enjoying all the pleasantries that Bishop's Bluff had to offer, Shane set his mind on finding a proper stable. Considering the number of horses about—Shane counted at least ten, mostly tied up at the saloon—the drifter thought that maybe there wasn't a horse lodge here after all. The thought alone was surprising given the town's clear plans for expansion. Already he could see construction on several other buildings farther up the street.

It wasn't much longer before he spotted a bright red barn just behind the hotel, and he rounded the two-story structure for a better look.

When Shane trotted up to the local stable, he was met with a large, wooden signpost plastered with ugly red lettering. "SAM'S STABLES," it read, with each "S" written backwards. "One-fifty a day."

That's highway robbery, Shane thought to himself, though he dismounted and knocked anyway.

At once, the large stable door swung open, and there stood a weathered old man with thick, cottony hair and a wooden stump in place of his left leg from the knee down. He flashed a quick smile at the stranger, which was largely toothless. Any pearls the man had left were rotting away by the hour.

"Afternoon, mister," he spoke, a shrill whistling sound trailing each word. "Name's Sam. You wanna stable yer horse, there?" He pointed to Shane's steed.

"That would be fine," Shane replied. "One-fifty a day?"

"You betcha. Got bills to pay, ya know. Gotta feed yer horses, ya know. Ain't much out this way. How long you gonna be stayin', mister?"

The gunslinger paused and took another gander at the small mountain town. He wasn't quite sure. Could be a week, could be a month. There was no telling how far north he dared go, so long as he never went any farther east.

When he was still a boy, Shane Cassidy was one of many who valiantly fought during the War Between the States. He couldn't say why he joined up initially. Perhaps it was the right thing to do, or maybe just the expected thing. He never saw much value in the conflict itself, but those around him certainly did. There was no real choice at all. But there was one thing that, by the end of it all, he was damned sure of: He would never step foot east of the Mississippi again.

For nearly twenty years, Shane had exiled himself to the western territories. He had spent some time down in Texas but soon pressed farther west and eventually north. He grew accustomed to the desert, where few of the men he once knew would think to follow. Though in time he grew sick of chapped lips, cracked skin, and endless chaparral. He hoped the cleaner air of mountain country would do him good.

So far, he was just cold.

"Not sure yet." Shane tossed Sam a small bag that jingled when the stable master caught it. "That'll cover at least a week." It wasn't a question.

Sam opened the bag, and a generous handful of silver dollars stared back at him.

"Y-Yessir. This'll work, sir. More than enough, sir."

Shane nodded and handed Sam the reins.

"Does he . . ." Sam stole a glance at the horse's undercarriage. "H-He have a name, sir?"

"No."

Shane didn't wait around to see that Sam took proper care of the animal. He could tell the man loved his horses when he offered a carrot before even getting the Thoroughbred through the large barn door. Shane understood the appeal. Horses were more agreeable than people and far easier to manage. Their needs were simple and their wants few. This beast was new to Shane, but the pair had formed a quick kinship, having learned to anticipate the movements of the other. He almost didn't mind paying a buck-fifty per day.

With his horse settled, the gunslinger set his eyes on the rest of Bishop's Bluff. Finding his way back to the main road, he could see that folks around here were used to strangers. Lumber seemed the primary occupation in these parts, though the corrals outside of town—about where the lone church stood—told another story. The smell of manure was inescapable. Shane concluded that the settlement was a frequent stop for longer cattle drives, likely for those taking stock all the way up to Montana or perhaps even Canada.

Nobody paid Shane Cassidy any mind as he climbed up the uneven road, and he liked it that way. The less attention he drew to himself, the better.

Shane's boots sunk deep into the muddy, wet snow as he trudged upward toward the saloon, anxious for a fast drink and a hot meal.

Before he was halfway up the road, he heard a shout from behind.

"Look, there he is!" called a lady from the hotel porch.

"Professor Knox is back," belted another behind the gunslinger.

Within minutes, every cowboy, homesteader, banker, and whore had gathered out in the slushy street around a bright, painted wagon that parked itself in front of the mercantile. It didn't look like much to Shane, who studied the red and yellow design sprawled on the side of the wagon. The colorful spirals on the sign, nailed almost perfectly to the side of the structure, bordered large, green lettering far more impressive than

Sam's penmanship. "Professor Knox's Miraculous Curative," it read, and suddenly, it all became clear.

The townsfolk crawled over one another to get to this makeshift shop on wheels. Shane thought it was like watching ants scramble across an anthill, crawling over one another with not a care in the world. With his stomach still set on a nice, hot meal, he marched past the commotion toward the saloon. Though he didn't get far.

"You, sir!"

Shane turned to see a bespectacled man with a trim suit and a top hat staring him in the face. The peddler, who had appeared almost out of thin air, wore a thick mustache that wisped at the ends. It was clear he'd gone unshaven for several days. The sharpness of his eyes beyond the glass paired with a familiar grin that Shane often saw on con men and bandits.

"What ailment troubles you, good sir?"

"Nothing troubles me," Shane replied.

"Nothing?" The man feigned a gasp. "A perfect man, then! We don't see many of you in these parts . . ."

Shane turned to leave, but the man's voice held him hostage.

"Sir, I am Professor Byron Knox, and you are in for a special treat." Knox produced a small bottle containing a dark, reddish elixir, presumably his miracle cure. Had Shane thought Knox was armed, he would've been buried in the snow. "I would like to offer you a bottle of my miraculous curative, free of charge."

"I'll pass."

"I wouldn't. You never know when you might find yourself in a gunfight." Knox looked over the gunslinger like a man window-shopping with a lady. A sly smile grew beneath his curled mustache. "A man like you, I can only assume, finds himself on the wrong end of a gun barrel quite frequently."

"That's where you're wrong," Shane said, finally looking the man in the piercing eye. "It's folks like you who find themselves on the wrong end of mine."

Knox let loose a half-hearted laugh.

"You see, my good people," the professor said, returning to his growing crowd, "some men be-

lieve themselves to be above even natural law.
While this curative will not keep you from death
forever, mind you, it *will* heal all wounds, ailments, and further bodily corruptions without
any effort on your part. Christ may save your
eternal souls, good people, but only Professor
Knox can mend your broken bodies!"

It was hard to believe that men like Knox could
exist in this part of the world and not starve
to death. Shane considered him nothing more
than a vulture, one who preys only on the weak,
needy, and desperate. There were surely more
than enough of those here.

As the faux medicine man continued to pro-
mote his medicine, Shane wondered how so
many could be so easily deceived. He counted at least two dozen men and women in the
crowd, with still more making their way over.
Knox was likely peddling nothing more than a wa-
tered-down stiff drink one could get far cheaper
at the saloon.

"How do we know this stuff works?" one older
fella shouted from the crowd.

"Yeah, why should we trust you?" spoke another.

"I am so glad you asked, my friends," Knox said with a bow. "Ling!"

Shane watched carefully as a short Chinese man dismounted from the front of the wagon, rushed right past him, and presented himself to the crowd. Knox placed a firm hand on the man's shoulder and flashed an enormous smile.

"Who would like to see a demonstration?" Knox asked. The eruptive response was clear, and so, moments later, Knox sent Ling into the middle of the street, his feet sinking in the mud.

"You see, good people of Bishop's Bluff, the only way to truly demonstrate the workings of this curative is by performing for you a true miracle. Healing a small ailment will only leave room for doubt, but my assistant, Ling, is here to cure your unbelief. You see, Ling has been shot countless times yet has not seen death. You may wonder how this is possible, but there is only one solution . . ." He raised a bottle of his curative, shaking it fervently. "Now, who will do me the honors of shooting this man once more?"

A heavy silence fell upon the townsfolk. Only moments ago, they had been as enthusiastic as Knox about the potential of his curative, but now, doubt had crept into each of their hearts.

"Not a soul?" the professor asked. "Folks, remember, we are professionals. Nothing you could do to Ling cannot be undone with but a drop of my miraculous curative. There is nothing to fear."

The man's words were not quite so reassuring as he may have hoped.

"What about you, friend?" he said, returning his crafty eye to Shane. "You said yourself that it's your barrel that folks should take heed of . . . How about it?"

"I'm not in the business of killing innocent men."

Knox sighed. He was beginning to lose his crowd. A concerned murmur rippled across the horde, and it was clear that drastic times called for far more drastic measures.

Without another word, Professor Knox marched to the back of his wagon and produced a shiny Peacemaker as if he'd conjured it from nothing. It all happened so fast that nobody could believe what they had just seen. A puff of black smoke burst in the air, and when it cleared, the peddler's companion lay motionless in the street.

Hell broke loose faster than a rattler in a gopher hole. One of the older church ladies fainted in the street as some of the younger men ran off to retrieve the absent sheriff. Others muttered amongst themselves, wondering if Knox could really pull off what he was selling. It didn't seem possible. He had gunned down that man right in front of them—there was no denying that—but it didn't seem to worry the professor at all.

Shane watched carefully as the swindler waltzed over to the man suffering on the ground.

"Now, now, look here, friends," Knox spoke, a firmness in his voice as if he were talking to a group of unruly school children. "Look here!" The chatter died down as all eyes fell on Knox. He removed a bottle from his breast pocket, unscrewed the lid, and poured the liquid down the man's throat. Ling was barely breathing but holding onto whatever life he had left. "It's only a matter of time."

The gunslinger wasn't sure what he expected to see when Professor Knox pulled the trigger. The pistol could have been merely filled with powder as at the theater, but he had seen the impact made on Ling's flesh. Everyone watched the blood splatter, and even now, some still trickled into the muddied snow beneath him.

And yet, when Professor Knox lifted his assistant up from the cold, wet ground, the man's color returned in full. Moreover, his breathing had returned to normal. He opened his shirt to reveal a small scar, right where the bullet hole would have been. It aligned perfectly with the hole torn through his clothes.

"I'm afraid my curative only works on living flesh and not clothing." Knox chuckled. "But it will have to do. My good people, you have just seen a man shut death's door and rid himself of the weight of eternity. Ling not only lives, but he walks now as if he had never been shot at all, save for a small scar, of course. But even Christ bore the marks of his crucifixion . . . Thank you, Ling."

Ling wasted no time returning to his place on the wagon as Knox marched to the back. The professor opened a cupboard to reveal a host of vials, each filled with his miracle solution. To the people of Bishop's Bluff, they may as well have been gold. Nearly every man and woman in the crowd fought to stake their claim with the professor, who suddenly had far more customers than spectators.

Shane was not one of them. He had had his fill of this insanity, and, while he couldn't explain what he had seen, he knew there was some sort of catch. There was no mistake about it, the cure-all was effective, but how? Why? These questions haunted Shane, though he tried to leave them behind.

As he reset his course for the saloon, Shane stopped at the front of Knox's wagon and peered over at Ling. The man sat stiller than a tombstone and looked about as uninterested in the land of the living as Shane imagined the dead were. Only, this man was very much alive.

"He shoot you like that often?"

Ling said nothing.

"Can't speak English?"

"I speak English just fine," Ling said, surprising Shane with little trace of an accent. The man looked down with a grim countenance plastered across his face.

"Good English, too. If you're so smart, how did you end up with that fraud?"

"Professor Knox is many things, but he is no fraud." Ling stopped his ominous staring and looked Shane square in the eyes. For a moment, they seemed to burn. "He is a master of the mystic arts. He holds the keys to death itself."

Shane Cassidy didn't stick around much longer. In fact, he spent the rest of his afternoon and much of the evening as a patron of the Silver Spur Saloon. Most of that time, he secluded himself in the back corner of the establishment, observing the cowboys and gamblers who spent their off-hours drinking themselves into a frenzy. He played a few hands of poker to indicate that he didn't pose a threat and enjoyed a warm meal of biscuits, beans, and a small steak that wouldn't have satisfied a dog. Shane wasn't one to complain. Any meal was better than none, especially considering the cold.

The evening sun had set early, and a frigid air fell upon Bishop's Bluff. It reminded Shane of the nights he spent out in the desert. As darkness fell and lamps were all lit, he noticed that some of the men who had wandered in were those he'd seen at Professor Knox's demonstration hours earlier. No doubt they had fallen for the con.

"Look here, Joe!" said one of them, a short fellow with a dark scar on his right cheek. "You remember how that old mule busted my foot last spring?"

"Sure," replied Joe, the barkeep. He scratched an itch on his chin and poured the man some whiskey. "You was hobbling around fer weeks. You still don't walk right."

"I do now!" The man took a quick lap around the floor, prancing like a pony, before thrusting his leg onto the bar. He removed his boot to reveal a dirty foot. "You see this? I used to have a big welt here the size of one of those steaks you serve here. Well, not anymore. Even better, there's not a lick of pain."

"How'd that happen, Bill?"

Bill looked Joe dead in the eye. "It was that miracle man, Joe. That Professor Knox. He's the one who cured me, and he can cure that bad back of yours, too. I know it." He slammed his drink down.

Joe waved Bill off and poured him another. "My back's just fine."

"No, it ain't, Joe. I know it ain't, and so do you." Bill gestured to the two friends he wandered in with, big guys built like lumberjacks. Shane assumed they probably were. "We've all tried the stuff. It's grand. Goes down smooth as this whiskey."

"Look, Bill, I'm glad it helped you. Really, I am. But I don't need any snake oil salesman comin' in here and pawning off some kooky curative when I've got all the medicine you'll ever need right here." Joe migrated to the other patrons at the bar, and Bill and his friends followed.

"What are you saying, Joe?"

"I'm not saying anything," Joe expressed. "I'm just saying I don't need it, is all."

"Oh, you're too good for it, is that it?"

Shane could see that things were about to turn ugly. It had been an occupational hazard over the years that he had been in enough saloons on enough cold nights to know how these sorts of things turn out. Bill would challenge Joe with some misplaced bravado, and Joe would kick him out. Or at least he'd try to. The pair would fight, and, considering his backup, Bill would probably win, only to leave on his own accord. He'd seen the same thing happen down in Prescott and again a week earlier in Salt Lake.

However, this time was different. There was something about this Bill character that made Shane uneasy.

"Look, Joe," Bill said, removing the bottle of Knox's curative he'd bought that afternoon. "You have just got to try it. Just a sip."

"I don't want it, Bill," Joe protested. "Now, if you aren't gonna buy another drink, then you might as well move on out."

Bill's men did just what Shane thought they'd do. They circled both ends of the bar, and the room got quiet. The piano playing had stopped, the card games took pause, and even the sporting girls upstairs had settled. Joe wore a frightened look on his face, and no one could blame him. In a panic, he drew his Sharps rifle from below the bar and waved it at those closing in. The gunslinger was impressed with Joe's stance. He was a man who knew how to handle a gun. Maybe they had once exchanged bullets in the war.

"I don't want any trouble here, Bill. You and your buddies get on out of here!"

The men didn't listen and instead continued to close in on the barkeep. They only stopped when Joe shot and crippled one and then did the same to the other. It was hard to tell from where Shane was sitting, but the way Joe handled his rifle led him to believe that the wounds were likely fatal. Both men nursed their injuries on the ground, but they weren't down for long. Each drank their own batch of Knox's special brand of healing elixir, and almost instantly, they were back on their feet.

One of the men thrust Joe high up off the ground with a single hand while the other broke the barkeep's Sharps over his knee. It was a powerful display of strength, Shane thought, and quite alarming.

What almost scared Shane Cassidy wasn't the seemingly supernatural strength of these men, or that they showed no signs of physical turmoil, but rather the blood-red shimmer in their eyes. Even from across the saloon, Shane could see that their eyes had shifted so that the whites were bloody. Even their pupils had a sheen to them that seemed to glow against the candle-light.

"Come on, Joe. It didn't have to be like this." Bill ascended the bar and addressed the onlook-ers around him. "Forget about what that preach-er has been saying, folks. Professor Knox is the real deal. It's more than just a cure-all; it's the way to a brand new life." He turned again to Joe, still held midair by his collar, and revealed his own bottle of unknown medicine. "You ready to see the light?"

Before Joe could answer, the bottle in front of him exploded like a powder keg in a warzone. Ire came over Bill, and he turned to the man responsible.

"Leave him alone," Shane said. He wasn't sure what possessed him to step in. He wanted to lie low here in town, and he had no intention of making new enemies. Yet, there was his Colt revolver, aiming squarely at this Bill character's face. "Next one will go through you unless you let that man alone."

"You must be new in town, friend . . ."

"I ain't your friend."

"You were at the demonstration today, weren't you?" A hint of recognition glistened in Bill's eyes. "Knox tried to get you to shoot that Chinaman, but you walked away."

"Put the man down, Bill."

"You have me at a disadvantage; I don't know your name."

Shane cocked the hammer. "I don't offer it so freely as you do. Put him down."

Bill signaled to his man to let Joe down, and he obeyed like a carefully trained hound. The two brutes walked out from behind the bar as Bill returned to ground level. "We're finished here."

As they neared the exit, Bill turned back to Shane, his own eyes now flashing red. The gunslinger grew uneasy looking at them. They looked too close to death. The cadence in Bill's voice changed too.

"Be seeing you, stranger."

Shane stuck around for another hour.

He figured the brumal air would dissuade the trio from waiting around for him. But it soon came time for Shane to turn in himself. After paying the barman, who sheepishly thanked him, the gunslinger traded the warmth of the Silver Spur for the unwelcome evening breeze, which passed like a dangerous whisper seeking to drive curious men to their doom.

Shane wasted no time standing there getting stiff. He was keenly aware of his surroundings as he crossed the road, and an uneasy feeling crept upon him. Though he checked up and down the main strip, he could not see another face staring back at him. The moon and the stars testified to the fact that he was the only one out at this hour. Everyone else was either at home by their fires or in the saloon, finding other ways to warm their bellies.

When Shane entered the Baker Hotel, he had no trouble securing a room on the second floor. Sleep came easily to him, though he didn't dream. In fact, Shane Cassidy hadn't dreamed in years. After the war, he had woken often in the night, drenched in a cold sweat, having relived the horrors he had seen on the battlefield. He almost wished that he had been pulled from a dream, because when he did abruptly awake in the night, he found two large paws grasping at his throat.

Though the man's hands were enough of a danger, what really caught Shane's eye were the two red beams staring back at him. Armed with a powerful glow, the man—the man who had broken Joe Kendall's Sharps over his knee—pressed his entire being on Shane.

Shane gasped and wheezed for air, but none came. The world around him brightened as a white fade crept in from all sides.

The gunslinger used all his might to roll the two of them onto the floor, breaking the larger man's hold over him. Unfortunately, the crash pushed Shane's revolver—which he had set on top of his boots—clear across the floor, and he wasn't quite quick enough to catch it. He crawled desperately towards his weapon, only to find himself shuffled backward instead. The lumberjack of a man grabbed Shane and, unencumbered by the gunslinger's weight or protest, tossed him across the room. The concussive slam rattled Shane, who was surprised he didn't go clean through the splintering wall.

Shane reached for the hidden blade he kept in his boot only to realize that it was still at his bedside. The revolver lay in the center of the room, and he was now slightly closer than his opponent. His feet were bare, and he could only hope to reach his firearm in time.

The red-eyed lumberjack charged toward Shane with a fierce anger. He could almost feel the heat emitting from the man's unnatural body. As Shane leapt toward his Colt, he nabbed the weapon just in time to get a shot off before he was surrounded by slivers of glass and a sudden chill. Suddenly, he was weighed down by an incredible pull, and the world around him went black.

When Shane Cassidy finally came to, he was covered in a few thick blankets and hungrier than a pack of wolves. He could barely see anything through his glossed eyes and wiped them until his vision returned. Beside him sat a lamp with a wily flame that fought the impulse to die out. He wasn't sure where he was, but he knew it wasn't heaven.

If it were hell, then it was a far better hell than he had envisioned for himself.

Shane tried to pull himself off the table he'd been placed on but was met with a barking pain that shoved him back down. He vowed not to try that again until he had mustered the strength to power through it. This failed attempt wasn't a complete waste, however, as the struggle caught the eye of a man fumbling in the darkness.

"Oh, you're awake!" he said. Soon, the older fellow—Shane guessed he was in his early fifties—stood above him, looking down with a compassion he had not seen up close in years. The white collar gave him away. "Land sakes, man. You took quite a tumble. If I hadn't happened by when I did, you would have bled to death in the street."

Shane could feel the stitches in his side. He could also still feel his arms and legs, which was a welcome surprise.

"W-Where am I?" he groaned.

"You're at the church, my friend. One of the first Baptist missions in the territory, in fact. Reverend Lawrence Harrison, at your service."

"Shane Cassidy," the gunslinger said with a faint nod. He looked for his Stetson, but it was nowhere to be found. "How do you do?"

"Far better than you, I'm afraid." The preacher seemed kind enough, and Shane didn't discern he was the dangerous sort, nor like the hypocritical, snobbish kinds he remembered from his youth.

"What happened?"

"Well," the minister began as he took a seat beside him, "I was hoping you might tell me. Seems only fair after I pulled you back here and dressed your wounds. You are going to be alright, by the way. That thick snowbank outside the hotel broke your fall."

"You a doctor, too?"

Shane meant the question in jest and was surprised when Reverend Harrison nodded. "The only one in town at the moment. Before the Good Lord called me into the service, I practiced medicine back east. Like the gospel writer Luke, I suppose He intended me to follow both my profession and my calling. You have a few minor lacerations, by the way. There will be some bruising and tenderness around those areas. I was able to stitch you up some, but I believe you may be suffering a fracture or two."

As the preacher spoke, Shane's memory flooded back to him. He soon remembered the man who attacked him in his sleep. The red eyes, the impossible strength. Then he remembered the fall itself.

"I-I was thrown out a window?"

"That is how it appears. By one of Bill Braeden's friends, I believe. A big, ugly fella."

Shane remembered him well. "I shot him."

"Did you? Well, I didn't venture upstairs to see how he turned out, but last I saw him from below, he didn't look too good himself."

"I'm sure he just took another swig of that cure-all." Shane tried to pull himself back up again, and as he did, he felt a twisting in his chest that was mighty worrisome. Every muscle and bone wanted to bury themselves in the floor, but he pushed himself to stand, despite the burning sensation that crawled up his back. He gritted his teeth and fought the urge to yell.

"Take it easy, my friend," the reverend ordered. He offered Shane a hand, but the gunslinger pushed it away. His first step was like walking on a block of ice, and it was then he remembered that his boots were still back at the Baker Hotel, lying idly at his bedside.

Reverend Harrison anticipated Shane's very thought and offered some further comfort. "I've already sent someone for your boots," he said.

"Who?"

"Sam Jefferson, I believe you've met."

"The stable master?" It hurt to laugh. "Bet he charged you two bucks."

The preacher laughed at that, and so Shane let the reverend help him to a nearby pew. The gunslinger only now looked out at the small church house, noticing the boarded windows and unfinished floor. There were certainly enough empty pews. A modest wooden pulpit stood at the front of the sanctuary, looking out over the entire one-room hall.

Shane wasn't sure how he ended up here. He understood the logistics of it, how the kindly reverend had brought him here to heal. But it was the chain of events that he couldn't shake. It seemed that trouble always found him, no matter if he were looking for it or not. The men from the saloon came to mind. Bill Braeden and his hulking friends. They were out of control, and clearly his performance at the Silver Spur had irked them something fierce.

"Reverend." He turned to the preacher, who took a seat beside him. "What do you know about this Professor Knox?"

"The miracle man?" The pastor shifted in his seat. "Well, I know his miracles are phony."

"What makes you say that?" Shane gruffed.

"Well, because . . . the power to instantly heal the sick, reset an injury. We don't possess the means to accomplish those sorts of feats, not with modern medicine, that is. I would know." Reverend Harrison thought more about it for a moment and continued. "Those miracles, those are things that only God can do. They are beyond our human limitations."

"I'm not so sure, reverend." Another surge of pain leapt up Shane's spine. "I've seen it work. Seen it with my own eyes."

"At the demonstration today? I heard about that."

"Not only at the saloon. That man, Bill. He and his friends, they all drank it. Two of them got right back up again after getting shot." Shane told the rest of the story but considered omitting the next part. He didn't want this man of God to think he was more fit for an asylum than a town such as Bishop's Bluff. However, something compelled him to speak on anyway. "All three of 'em had eyes that glowed like the red sun at noonday. They switched with a blink." He turned to the pastor, who seemed to believe him. "Knox did it. I don't know how, but he made monsters out of these men. The one who attacked me tonight, he threw me clear across the room. It wasn't hardly an effort for him, not like me getting off that table."

The reverend paused for a moment, as if he were studying over the Good Book. Shane couldn't help but wonder if it made any more sense to the preacher than it did to him. These men had all been normal this morning but were now hostile, aggressive. They had amassed a power beyond mortal man, and they wielded it as if it had always been part of them.

"You know, after the demonstration this morning, there was something different about certain folks," Reverend Harrison admitted. "Sally McMurtry, for instance. She and Molly Horner got into an argument at the mercantile. They were calling one another all sorts of horrible, un-Christian names before I finally had to step between them. When I did, I could have sworn that Sally's eyes flashed red." Shane could hear the disbelief in the preacher's voice, but he spoke on anyway. "I don't know if Molly had taken any of that Knox's curative, but if I know Sally McMurtry, she did for certain. All these years complaining about a sore toe must've finally gotten to her."

"Preacher, we need to find out what's in those bottles."

"I couldn't agree more, son."

Just then, the big doors opened and shut, permitting a burst of cold air to rush through the chapel. It was Sam, and he'd brought Shane's boots.

"Mister, I am glad to see you awake. Now, you'll be happy to know that your horse is taken care of," the man said as he hobbled over to the gunslinger. "Now you are too."

"I didn't have any doubt," Shane replied.

"Sam, did you happen to see that Professor Knox today? The man with the wagon in town?" Reverend Harrison asked.

"Why, yessir, I did. He came to the stable and offered me a bottle of his curative, free of charge, he said." The preacher and the gunslinger exchanged troublesome looks, and Sam began to cower. "Did I do something wrong, reverend?"

"No, Sam. Not at all." He put a firm hand on the stable master's shoulder. "Did you drink any?"

"Well," Sam began, "the professor told me to. He said if I took just a sip, that my leg would be restored. Imagine that. But, you see, reverend, I was in the middle of shoeing horses, and I don't like to mix my work with pleasure, you see. So I told him I would have some right after I was done with work. Only, by the time I finished, I plum forgot. But now I'm wondering if I should talk to a doctor first. Say, you're a doctor, ain't you, reverend?"

"God bless you, Sam," the reverend said with a smile far more handsome than the horseman's. He quickly urged Sam to retrieve the bottle from the stable without daring to take a swig himself.

He told Sam that the curative was poisoned, and that wasn't a lie. From what Shane could see, Knox's medicine had only harmed the citizens of Bishop's Bluff. It may have cured their physical ailments, but it was an intrusive plague on their souls.

When Sam returned, barging in through the doors and letting more cold air seep in, he let out a shout and dropped the bottle.

"My hand!"

The reverend sprung to attend to Sam, whose hand had been strangely burned. The bottle had darkened his flesh, which emitted a whiff of smoke. Shane knelt to examine the bottle. He hurt all the way down.

From up close, Shane could see the dark, red liquid pulsing within the clear glass. It looked almost as if it were boiling, a strange reaction he couldn't understand. When he went to pick it up for himself, the bottle was far too hot to the naked touch. So, he used the sleeve of his jacket to keep from getting burned.

The mark on Sam's hand wasn't too severe, but it wasn't to be ignored either. Reverend Harrison bandaged it quickly to ensure the stable master didn't scratch at it. After his doctoring, he turned to the curative. As the learned minister examined the bottle, he was cautious. Shane could tell that the curious reaction occurring beneath the glass disturbed him.

"Where did you store this, Sam?"

"It's been sitting in the stables all afternoon," Sam replied. "It never got hot like that 'til I walked on in here."

"Curious," was all the reverend said.

Using his handkerchief, he took hold of the bottle and unscrewed the lid. He let slip a drop from the bottle, but when it splashed on the church house floor, the elixir evaporated. It didn't even stain. He tested this reaction again, and then again for a third time. Each attempt was more baffling than the last.

Satisfied with the experiment, Reverend Harrison marched outdoors and poured a few drops into the snow. This time, the curative remained a liquid and mixed into the white powder below. He tested this again to the same result. Then he ran up to the Baker Hotel, presumably to try it again there. When he returned to the church, he repeated the experiment thrice more, each time performing the same smokey result.

"This is troublesome," he concluded.

"What is it, preacher?" Shane growled.

"Medically speaking, I haven't a clue," the pastor admitted. "It is unlike any form of drug I have ever seen. I thought that, perhaps, the curative reacted negatively to warmer environments. Outdoors it remained a liquid, but in here, it turned to gas. However, it remained a liquid at the hotel as well." He plopped the lid back on the bottle and placed the solution into his coat pocket.

"What does that mean?"

"Well, it means that, as a pastor, I believe this is perhaps something more sinister. I'm afraid that it may be the work of the Devil himself."

Before Shane Cassidy had the chance to counter the reverend's theory, the minister spoke up once more.

"Mr. Cassidy, I don't know you from Adam, and you don't owe me nor this town a thing, but I implore you ... you seem to be the type of man who has dealt with men like this Knox before. I know you are injured, and if there were another man for the job, I would ask him. Our sheriff is useless, I'm afraid. If I know him, he has likely tasted this forbidden fruit for himself already. This leaves only you. Please find this man and drive him far away from here. If this spreads, there is no telling the damage that will be done.

"Who knows? Maybe this is why you found your way here in the first place."

Despite his wounds, Shane didn't much mind the ride out to the Connors homestead. Reverend Harrison had overheard Pete Connors offering Professor Knox a place to camp for the night, on the edge of their land just beside a small creek.

It was exactly where Shane found him.

Stopping at the edge of the tree line that broke into a small field, Shane could see Knox's wagon clearly. A small fire rested beside the shop-on-wheels, and it appeared that Knox was there alone. It would be best to travel the rest of the way on foot.

Sam had a spare case of ammunition for emergencies, and so he'd offered the gunslinger a few extra bullets. Though he wouldn't be much use right now in a physical brawl, Shane knew that, if he played his cards right, he could feign the strength to make the peddler believe he was a threat.

It was a quiet night, as countless snowflakes eased down to the earth. Shane was careful as he marched slowly through the powder. Way out here, away from the bustle of town, it was quite beautiful. This was the sort of country that Shane had come to long for in the desert. Now that he was here, it was just more of the same. Each step hurt worse than the last, but he had promised to see this through, and Shane Cassidy was a man of his word.

As he got closer to the wagon, he could hear what sounded like several voices communing with Knox beside the fire. Some were deep, while others gave off a high-pitched ring that was almost more irritable than the pain in his back.

Shane crouched down behind the wagon to see if he could garner a better look.

What he saw haunted him.

Knox was settled into the snow, but it wasn't a fire that he sat beside. Instead, the flaming symbol pulsed brighter than the stars, and from it sang the multitude of voices with whom the professor seemed quite acquainted. Far more disturbing was the skeletal corpse that sat just beside the professor, with bones that had been licked clean by God-knows-what sort of demon. A trail of blood led into the strange mark in the ground as if it had been chewed up and spit out.

Shane figured that there was no point in concealing himself any longer. He rose and walked up behind the man, who was bottling portions of the blood-soaked, ethereal flame in front of him.

"So this is how you do it?" Shane said, breaking the silence by cocking the hammer on his Colt.

"Evening, gunslinger." Knox didn't even look up. It was so cold that Shane could almost see the words form above the professor's head with each breath. He didn't seem the least bit worried. "I heard you found trouble this evening."

"Not as much as you're in, Knox. What is this poison? Good men are turning cruel, and even the ladies aren't all themselves."

"It's moving along faster than I'd hoped then."

The professor continued to fill his bottles with the strange essence creeping off the glowing symbol. Shane could now see that it was a five-pointed star, burned into the ground and surrounded by a shimmering ring of fire. Beneath it lay only scorched earth and blood.

"I arrive to bring these unsuspecting yokels a miracle, which they accept after a quick demonstration—thanks for nothing, by the way. Once they take my curative, their minds are fogged so masterfully that every inhibition and work of conscience is forcibly extinguished. Word spreads, and soon my acolytes force the poison down others' throats as well. Of course, it doesn't work for all, but it works for enough. The town tears itself apart, and the rest of the world thinks that a plague of some kind has consumed them. Of course, they're right."

"Why?" Shane asked in anger. "What do you get out of this?"

Knox smiled. "Everything. I'm going to be a king, you see. That's what they promised."

"'They,' who?"

Knox gestured to the pentacle. "'They,' they. Them. That Legion from the great beyond. God gave up on us long ago, leaving the rest to them. Now, they do with you people as they please."

Shane had kept his revolver on Knox the whole time, and the man couldn't have cared less. He kept babbling about power and money as if they were the only two things in the whole world, the only things that would secure his future.

"You see, my friend, their power runs through me, too. Only, unlike the chattel who are slaves to their impulses, I master myself. I have the powers of a god, and yet I live as a man, humbly on this mortal plane."

"Yeah, you're a regular messiah."

"Yes." The professor beamed. "All those years in academia, studying business and history and medicine, and for what? That's not where true power lies."

"No, true power lies with those who are willing to use it. It's time to run along now, professor. You're no longer welcome here."

"I think you're mistaken, gunslinger. It is you who are not welcome."

Out of the corner of his eye, Shane saw a slight movement in the snow.

It could have been Knox's mule wandering the grounds, but the gunslinger knew better. When Shane turned, he bent his knees and fell to the ground, positioning himself to avoid a bullet wound. He winced at the fire that once again flared up his back but held his Colt steady as he turned.

When he pulled the trigger, he watched as Ling's body jerked back with force. He hit the man right between the eyes, stopping him cold. Ling's pistol—the same one that Knox had used earlier that day—fell somewhere in the snow.

Anticipating an attack from behind, Shane turned again, his knee steadying him in the snow. Knox hadn't moved.

"An impressive display of violence," Knox said as he clapped. "Truly marvelous. Where did you learn such fantastic gunplay?"

Shane cocked the hammer once more. "No more games, Knox. It's time to go."

"It's a shame about Ling. He had a family, you know. He was hoping to earn enough working here with me that he could send for them back east. It's a shame, really. Oh well, I will find another desperate soul willing to tag along."

Shane slowly pushed himself up from the ground. He thought on the man he had just killed and how he wished it hadn't come to this. He thought about how he wished the reverend had never asked him to come here. But mostly, he thought about Knox. He knew the man wouldn't stop, that he would continue to harass town after town, that he would turn good people into monsters.

It was that thought that spurred Shane Cassidy to pull the trigger.

Any power that Professor Byron Knox thought he had vanished the moment he hit the ground. Swarmed by the primordial inferno he had summoned, the professor was pulled into a realm that Shane could not understand. The gunslinger thought he saw a scaly hand reach around Knox as the man used his final breaths in this world to scream.

With a horrible flash, the portal was gone, and Shane was left alone.

After setting fire to Knox's wagon, Shane rode back into town. He brought Ling's body to the church and asked Reverend Harrison to see that the man was buried and that his family was notified. Then he handed the minister all the cash he collected from Knox's wagon and prompted him to send it along as well.

"You killed him?" the reverend asked. "Knox, I mean."

"He killed himself," Shane replied. "I was just the unlucky one who delivered the message."

"It's over then?"

"I burned his supply, but folks here had bought him out beforehand."

"I don't think that's going to be a problem," Reverend Harrison revealed. He handed Shane the bottled curative they had examined earlier. To his surprise, it was cold to the touch, even here in the church. "I believe whatever dark power it once held was extinguished with Knox."

Shane nodded. "It was their power to begin with."

"Whose?"

"You said it yourself, reverend. This was the Devil's work, and he always comes to collect."

As Shane turned for the door, the preacher called back to him.

"If you weren't here, I believe this would have ended very differently."

Shane remained silent.

"What I'm saying is, thank you."

The gunslinger nodded and then left the church house.

THE COTTON EYED KILLER
BY: ROSS CARMONA

1

"Cazadoras?" Sheriff Harlow said, eyeing the women across his desk.

They still had dust on their coats from the trail and watched him with the look of two hardened contractors looking for work. On the desk between them lay the flyer. The letters pressed in a large font, the bounty numbers and the name of the wretch standing out like black towers in a sea of yellowed parchment. Yet where a portrait of the wanted man was usually framed there was only a blank space. He knew the paper well; he had sent them out years ago when the madness started, a descent that had only sped up with time.

The pair across from him were two of the strangest drifters to ever saunter through his door. The one who did most of the talking was a blonde woman in a black dress and corset that clung to her body like a second skin. The way she smiled, the way she talked without saying much, and the way she made him want to listen told him she was trouble. And if this woman was trouble, then her partner was that twice over.

The other woman was tall and lean, dark red hair spilling across her shoulders and down her back. She wore a white button-up with a bandana around her neck to keep away the dust while riding. She had jeans that looked like they'd seen a thousand miles of hard travel and a pair of oiled, gleaming revolvers strapped to her thighs in low-hanging leather holsters. She'd had on a wide-brimmed leather hat pulled low to shade her face when she'd entered, and it had taken his prodding for her to remove it. It didn't take much to see why. Her skin had a deep cerulean tint, a hue of blue somewhere between the sky on a crisp day and the shade of a sapphire. She was a Shai, one of the forgotten tribes scorched from the earth during the civil war. She regarded him with eyes like glowing cinders, a shade of red close to blood.

When this woman spoke, she cut straight to the point. Words striking him square as though she'd drawn one of her guns and fired it at him. " My name is Yami, and she is June. We have come for your Cotton-Eyed Killer."

"Been a long time since any of your kind came through. What makes you believe I still need your help?" he asked, chest puffed out and jaw set.

"Have you walked outside?" June asked, gesturing out the window. One look was enough. Windows of shops either boarded up or smashed completely open, the glass of the panes left to pollute the decaying boardwalk running along the buildings. Bloodstains dried across the steps. No people on the street, no carts, no horses tied to hitchings, not even water in the trough in front of his office. "Seems like you lot hardly have a leg to stand on."

The words stung, but he bit down the impulse to shout back. She spoke with a city accent he knew well from his days back east, back when he and his family still lived near the sprawling hell of roaring industry. Years before he'd dragged his wife and daughter out here to a different kind of hell, a place not unlike a trap set out for a fly. A pitfall you never noticed until you were already sinking in the vinegar. Harlow breathed a deep sigh, feeling the weight of many sleepless nights on his shoulders.

"His name is Joe . . ."

2

"No one knows where he came from, or where exactly he goes. We only know that he appears on the night of the Cutter's Moon," Harlow said as Yami studied the heavy bags under his eyes, and the tremble in his hands. "When the moon casts a greenish glow, and not a star is visible, he comes on the wind."

"'Twas several years ago now, when it first started, on the eve of a feast for the harvest. The streets were full back then, all of the townies either drunk on corn wine or high on life's cheer. I had just moved here with my wife Liza, our daughter Isa, and her fiancé Dillon . . ." Harlow's voice took on a deep sorrow, a haze clouding his eyes. "I took over the badge and deputized the boy, gave him a wage to support what was to be a coming family. Little good it did him in the end."

Yami watched Harlow reach to the side of his desk, pulling a bottle of brandy from his drawer and a single glass cup. He didn't offer as he poured, only continuing, "I was beside him when it happened, both of us watching our women dance in the street under the glow of the lanterns, all while a band played a tune that echoed across the town. I can still remember Liza holding Isa in her arms as they turned, smiles on their faces . . ."

"Then there was a whirlwind; it came on us fast. Kicked up so much dirt it sent dust clouds spilling across the valley. The sight was unlike anything I've ever seen. Not like any black blizzard the locals ever had either," Harlow said, his gaze now fixed on the farthest wall like he was watching the scene unfold. "In a moment the whole town was covered in heavy green clouds that ate everything they touched."

Looking out the window Yami could imagine the event. The sky turning an apocalyptic emerald as everything faded into a haze. People vanishing in the dust's embrace. She was turning back to focus on Harlow when she spotted someone outside, a figure across the street leaning on a support beam holding up the awning running along the boardwalk. Yami had spied a few people coming and going on the street when she and June arrived. None of whom looked like they wanted to be seen, all of them scurrying with the disposition of mice expecting a cat. This girl was different. The wind sent her dark hair swirling. She had a light brown face, a complexion not unlike Harlow's, and looked to be in her mid-twenties. She stared directly at Yami, her deep brown eyes searching her soul. As an instant passed between them, the Blue Lady felt a chord of memory echo across her heart. The girl had her arms folded across her chest and a bemused smile spreading across her face.

"In that wall of darkness," Harlow said, not dropping a beat in his story or acknowledging Yami's distraction, "I heard a voice speak to me, and I've heard it every night in my dreams since. It laughed and left every hair on my spine wired . . ."

Yami perked up at this, motioning for June to get out her notes. The woman in black did so, winking quickly as she withdrew a small pad and pen from her bodice. "What did it say exactly? Can you remember?"

A look of discomfort passed on Harlow's face, a look that could have been resistance at remembering the past. "It was a long time ago. I only recall parts of it . . ." Harlow said, a flush brightening his cheeks, his eyes studying the grooves on his desk from where he'd been gripping the edge.

"Try," Yami said, her voice flat as hardpan.

The Sheriff gritted his teeth, and said:

"'*Rest easy lawman, for you may keep
your life.
Soon you shall taste mine own strife.
This promise to you, I will make.
It is everything you love I shall take . . .*'"

When the man was done, he looked like a drinker who'd reached the end of the bottle and bitten the worm.

June's face brightened, her pen scribbling as she said, "He speaks in rhyme, eh? Peculiar. How do you know his name is Joe?"

Once again, a look of uneasiness filled the sheriff's face, however this time it was only a momentary passing and was quickly replaced with rage. "I know because he told us! I know because this demon has haunted our town for years and sapped away our strength! When the dust clouds parted I found Liza in my daughter's arms, and the boy not far from them."

He rose from his seat as he spoke, his voice filled with so much force that June recoiled as if she'd just faced a barking dog on a chain. Yami, however, didn't budge as much as she just leaned back in her chair, arms folded across her chest. The man looked from one of them to the other, his voice growling as he continued, "Their bodies were so twisted and mangled that I could hardly recognize them. And their eyes . . . he left their eyes as white as cotton, as white as bone. As though whatever they saw destroyed them before he did . . ."

Silence then, nothing but the creaking of the building around them before Harlow said, "We buried them after, along with a half dozen others taken that night. My Isa hasn't spoken to me since . . ."

"Odd he left your daughter alive." June stated, her voice carrying the hint of a question.

"He did so to torment me." Harlow said, "Every night since he's held the threat of her life over me, the threat of coming back and taking what I have left. I hear him in my dreams . . ."

"Seems petty punishment without cause." Yami said.

A look passed over Harlow's face, an emotion far colder than the anger he'd presented so far, yet not without an edge. For a moment Yami believed he looked more statue than lawman, and it was only a deep breath and a bitter smile that told her he hadn't frozen. He was calm when she spoke next, to the point, "I know not the machinations of spirits. That is your specialty. The creature staved off more death if we gave him offerings. Coins in our purses, food from our tables, wine from our bottles," Harlow said, his tone dropping once more to a passing calm. "However . . . when we have nothing to give, or even too little, he takes one of us. Pulls someone screaming from their bed in the night and leaves the mutilated corpse in the street by sunrise. Nothing but their cotton-white eyes left staring. And . . ."

"Your money has dried up." Yami said, it wasn't a question.

Red of face, and undoing his collar, the sheriff only nodded as he sat back down. He poured another drink, and only after he'd downed the shot did he say, "Aye. I thought foolishly that I could get someone to take care of the problem. I pooled money for a bounty, sent out posters, wrote to the judge of the territory for aid, but the call went unanswered."

"If you still have that bounty, we'll find a way," June said. "The next Cutter's Moon is at the end of the week."

"Then we have a deal."

3

"You don't think it's some kind of localized haunting? Demonic even?" June asked, sucking down her cigarette like it was running away.

She leaned against the railing along the board-walk on the high street, wind blowing through her blond locks, Yami beside her. Some of the houses around them had lights glowing through the windows, but the majority did not. After exiting the sheriff's office—the old man had taken his time to point out the hotel down the street before walking off to his own home, his shoulders slumped—neither woman had seen much of anyone.

"The wind and the way it talks implies it's some spirit, but there's something else there. The sheriff didn't help much."

"He said what he wanted." Yami leaned on the rail, a jar of the red powder in her hands. She had been weighing it since pulling it from her satchel, feeling the curved glass in her palm and deciding if she had enough to keep them both alive. She knew she'd need to work on the exact measurements when they both made it to the hotel and got a room.

"Fine man. He's like a brick wall. Hard to move and dull as stone," June said, puffing a cloud of tobacco. "But if his money's good I don't mind."

Yami grunted. A week back they had been posted up in the capital of the territory, a town somewhere between the conveniences of civilization and the desolateness that ruled the desert. Late one night June hadn't returned from an evening at the saloon, and it set Yami's nails on edge. She stomped over and found that her light-fingered friend had lost more than a few hands at cards and was failing to talk herself out of the ensuing repercussions. Said repercussions were three large men with biceps as big as her head and little but anger in their dark eyes.

Yami had watched June sweat a minute, savoring the visual of long-delayed comeuppance. Ultimately she intervened before fists could fly, taking hold of the biggest man's wrist and twisting sharply till she felt a pop. Everyone who saw her knew she was a Shai—as clear as the color on her face—but few knew that even the weakest of her people was still stronger than most men. There had been some crying and some threats, but in the end they came to an agreement: pay the debt back in a month's time, with interest, and all would be like water under bridges. The only problem was that they had yet to find stable work in several months. This job was supposed to solve those problems, yet Yami had doubts.

"Does starin' at that stuff tell us where we're gonna find this cotton-eyed bastard?" June said, elbowing Yami's side.

"Going for a walk," Yami said, shoving the jar back into her pack and turning away from June, back down the boardwalk toward the eastern road out of town. "Check on the horses before you rent a room." The last place they'd left their two mares was in the stable across from the Sheriff's office, in the gloved hands of a groom with a bad hairline and worse breath.

Yami walked without much idea where she was going or what was compelling her. She only knew that there was a pull within her that wouldn't release its hold. As she strolled along the dirt road she could feel the unseen eyes watching her. The sun was setting, and lights in the windows of houses she passed shimmered like candles at a funeral. Out of the corner of her eye she could make out the shifting of shapes at the curtains, faces peeking from cover. They were marking her, deciding if she might bring some hope of change or just end up in another grave.

Eventually the road thinned, the houses diminishing until there were only a few run-down shacks on the outskirts. Here, Yami could take in a wide view of the valley, of the desolate hardpan that stretched from one horizon to the other, broken up only by the swell of mountains putting the town in their shadow. As the wind blew between the cracks of the rocks and swept across her face and past her ears, kicking up trailing locks of her hair like fire streaming, she heard a call on the wind, a whistle. She scanned the horizon, looking for another sign, until she spotted a spark of light at the end of the road, near the great tree she and June had passed on the ride into town. It flashed twice.

By the time she arrived at the base of the tree the sky had shifted over into a black blanket filled with pinpricks of white. The moon was beginning to appear from its hiding place, a greenish eye opened to reveal a black sliver running in a vertical curve that would only grow darker in the days to come. The Cutter's Moon. A time of bad omens, a time of broken oaths and promises betrayed, so stories told. As she walked Yami tried not to pay it mind. She only studied the flickering light beneath the tree, a lantern's glow.

She found the lantern hanging from one of the lowest branches of the bone white tree, its spindling limbs reaching up to the sky with clawing leafless fingers. It had been long petrified by the desert, the heat stealing all the color from it but none of its sheer size. In the days it was truly alive, years or even decades ago, it must have been a sight. Beneath the lantern, there sat the kneeling figure of a young woman dressed in white, her head bowed, hands clasped together.

The lantern's light illuminated the hanging shapes on the lowest branches of the tree, figures that Yami had only paid a passing glance at on the ride earlier, figures she told herself she wanted to get a better look at when she got the chance. They were talismans, some crude crosses made of sticks tied together like you might find on a grave marker, items of significance to whoever had put them there: a child's drawing, a wedding ring, a lock of hair. Yami even spotted a lady's shoe hanging from one branch, its weight causing the wood to bend but not break.

"It's called a memento tree," said the girl. Yami's eyes shifted to her, the girl wore a white sundress and had dark skin that almost blended into the night. "It honors those taken from us."

Yami stared at the girl a moment, something about her prickling in the back of her mind. She had a youthful face and smiled an enigmatic grin that touched only the corner of her lip and said more than Yami ever could with whole sentences.

"Back home we had a similar practice," Yami said, locking eyes with the girl as she rose to her feet and brushed off the dust on her knees. "Outside my not-father's homestead, his family had one planted to remember their kin."

"Was this with the Shai?" the girl asked, cutting right to the bone and not worrying about bringing up any memories that might distress the Blue Lady. After all, how could she know?

Yami smiled a bitter grin and said, "No, I was only ever with my tribe as a babe. By the time I was two summers all who bore me were dead, and a ranger passing through had adopted me as his own."

"Your not-father?" the girl asked.

Yami nodded.

There was silence between them then. It was always so easy for June to talk, a trait Yami envied. Before the silence could stretch on much longer, the girl said, "Sorry, I shouldn't have pried. Look at me getting you talk about yourself and not even givin' my name. Isa Harlow."

Yami's eyes grew just a little wider at the realization. The girl did have some of the same features as the sheriff, when you were looking for them. From the shape of the nose to the color of the eyes and tint of skin. Though she was at least twenty years his junior, the resemblance was there. But that wasn't where she knew the girl, and that fact only grew louder in her mind; more immutable.

"You and that pickpocket think you can really take on Joe?" Isa asked, leaning against the bark of the tree and crossing her arms over her chest. "The last folks who tried that ended up spread across town in a dozen pieces."

"He is not the first monster we have killed. He will not be the last." Yami said, looking at Isa's bemused face and still reading her like a book without a title. "How did you know June?"

Isa laughed, but only a chuckle escaped her lips. "Haven't placed me yet? Don't remember?" Isa kept smiling, a playful spark in her eye.

Yami tried to let a smile creep on her face as well, but she had to force it. The girl was pretty, yet she felt an uneasiness looking at her, a sensation like biting into a perfectly ripened apple and fearing the worm hiding within.

Yami shook her head slowly, not breaking eye contact. The fact that the girl hadn't looked into those eyes with fear told her they must have met before. Only those who had seen her eyes up close and personal—the way they almost seemed to glow with a light all their own in the dark of night, like two smoldering coals—had ever accepted them.

"I'm not surprised; you seemed mighty busy at the time. Essonberg, midsummer, four years back. You were dealin' with them O'Hara brothers," Isa said, and the moment she mentioned the town, everything began to click. "I was workin' the register the day those rabid scoundrels pulled a gun on me. Hardly noticed at the time 'cause I was too busy watchin' your partner pickin' a fine gentleman's coat pocket in the shop aisle. I was 'bout to holler her way, tell her to scram or I'd call the law, when suddenly I was starin' down the barrel of a big iron."

Yami recalled the day well. She and June had taken the contract from the town mayor, a skittish man who always looked like he was a door slam away from a heart attack. The city had been under constant siege by two of the nastiest half-men bandits to ever stalk the hills. Brothers born with the skin of beasts and bloodlusts to match. An easy enough job; all they had to do was blend in and wait for an opportunity. For June that always meant tailing a few marks.

"I swear I was countin' the seconds down to judgement day while they was barkin' at me to empty the register." Isa said, looking down at her dusty shoes disappearing in the growing dark. "But then I heard you call out their names, and there was fear in those boys' eyes when they turned on you. The shots are still echoing in my ears now . . . I've never seen anyone draw so fast . . ."

Yami shrugged and shuffled in her boots. "I got lucky. You usually do in a gunfight."

"No, you were good. They had their guns drawn and didn't even get to pull a trigger before you had them on the floor," Isa said, looking into Yami's eyes with a tenderness that felt foreign.

"But they were just men, even if half. Whatever Joe is, he's worse."

Yami was about to speak, but she was cut off as Isa continued.

"My fiancé was a lawman like my daddy. He was fast too. So good with a gun he ended up coming out here followin' my daddy because we wanted a family," Isa explained, looking off and away from Yami, no tear in her eyes, only a deep sadness. "Would have been married a long time ago, if not for Joe . . ."

There was silence then, nothing between them but the wind howling as it raced across the desert and sent the mementos on the tree to dance.

"After the O'Hara brothers were gettin' their blood all over my boss' nice clean floor, you came over and helped me up," Isa said, "You took me out of the shop while others stood around gawkin' and your partner ran off to get the watchman. It was kind."

Yami said nothing, she just shuffled again in her boots, unable to find any words. It was her curse. Talk had never come easy, even in the best of circumstances.

She was about to open her mouth and say something, anything to fill the space between them, but Isa raised a finger and said, "I know your type. You remind me of my Will. He could never speak his mind, even when I tried to wring it out of him."

Yami shook her head, running her fingers through her hair. "Your father is not telling me everything." She explained the story Harlow had told her, noticing the way the girl's face didn't so much as change, as the look on her own face grew darker by the moment.

When the recounting was over Isa smiled. It was a pained look, but she took a step closer and ran her fingers down Yami's sapphire cheek. "It's not a pretty tale."

Yami put herself against the tree, feeling the bark dig into her shoulder as she stared down at Isa. "Tell me."

"I ain't spoken to Daddy since it happened, not since the storm. But he's a fool to not tell you about Joe." Isa said, close enough that her breath warmed the space between them. "Joe didn't come outta nowhere. No, he was a man once, before whatever he is now. And a charmer if ever there was one.

"There was no keepin' him away from the ladies in town when he first stepped off the coachline dressed in a fine tailored suit. Said he was a travelin' man, and there wasn't a thing he couldn't sell you. That first night he must have had close to a dozen women talkin' in his ear at the banquet in the hall. The next night, double that."

"That must have upset the men," Yami said.

Isa nodded, studying the Blue Lady's profile. "Aye, and by the end of that week there was dark talk in the saloon. Will said that it was all huff and puff, but I was never sure . . ."

"What did they do to him?" Yami asked, turning her gaze back on the girl, her eyes still smoldering with their nightglow.

Isa's face fell, her smile gone. "Not sure. I only know that the night before the Cutter's Moon my Daddy and lot of the men started walkin' out of town. Will followed and wasn't back for a long time. I stayed up sittin' by the door, waitin' to see if any of them would come back. It wasn't till sunrise that Will got back. He didn't tell me what they was doin' out there. He just said that Joe was gone."

"But he was never really gone . . ." Yami said.

Isa shook her head, a tear forming in her eye. She didn't turn away from the Blue Lady then, she just took another step closer and wrapped her arms around her. "Not till the storm that night, not till the wind . . ."

They were there under the tree a long while before heading back to town.

4

The next morning June was up on Yami's orders, talking to every townie who would see her and taking 'donations' from whoever would give them. When June complained that the latter might be a little difficult, Yami only replied, "Get what you can. Silver coins only. I will take the eastside." With that, the Blue Lady was in the wind.

By the time they met each other again, it was close to sundown. The town hall was serving food, dinner for a dime, and the two sat at a table far away from the prying eyes of any looking to snoop. Haggard-faced men and women stared their way with tired eyes, gazes that looked at them like two bugs crawling in the dirt. June remembered just how well her collections had gone and massaged the place at the back of her head where a crone nailed her with a rock as she ran.

Sitting across from Yami, the woman digging into a bowl of poor man's stew like it was evaporating, June couldn't help but notice the dust on her clothes, and the sweat on her brow.

"You look like you did better than me," June said, using her spoon to stir the mixture of broth and vegetables cooked down to the point of mush. "This isn't exactly the best town to go around asking for money."

"How much you get?" Yami asked between spoonfuls.

June shrugged and bit her lower lip. "Two silver spots, and I'm not sure one of them isn't painted." She withdrew the coins and tossed them on the table.

"It will have to do," Yami said, removing two of her own coins from her pocket. June started, but Yami only raised her bowl and drank the last of her broth.

For the next few days, right up to the evening of the Cutter's Moon, the two were busy. They took up residence in the abandoned blacksmiths shop and used the last of their spare cash to buy coal for the forge from a retired miner named Bill who hoarded the stuff in a hut on the edge of town. A day into their work, Isa appeared at the door and asked how it was going. One look at their work and she had little but confusion on her face.

"You two think all this is gonna work?" Isa asked, leaning over Yami working with the molten metals.

"It must."

The night of the Cutter's Moon arrived with a foul wind in the air and the descent of a greenish haze across the valley. The storm came, appearing out of nothing and growing in size. Wildlife looked towards the coming catastrophe and ran far. People in their homes hid under bedspreads and shuddered as a chill racked them. When he awoke to the world there was already hate in his heart, a fire that only grew with a sound on the wind. The sound of music played, the rhythm of a band playing a jaunty tune.

He descended, moving the force of a storm wall across the valley, bringing a veil of blackness, devouring all he touched. Houses in his path were torn to splinters, trees were uprooted and sent crashing back to earth, any life caught in his whirlwind was rendered to crimson mist. Despite the anger, he was pleased, pleased that they had finally given him a reason to collect what he was owed. It had been weeks since the last offering, and while many in town had paid with blood, there was one prize he had staved off collecting. He had played the game too long, taken too much time with them. That daughter was still here, one last fruit on a rotting tree.

When he arrived in town, hovering over the dark streets and calming his winds just enough to peer into the dim windows, all seemed as dead as ever; all seemed stripped of hope. For a moment he mulled his mistake, considering if he'd been led astray. Yet, in the center of the street, standing out like a star on a moonless night, were the blazing open windows of the town hall. The doors were cracked ajar and from it escaped that frustrating, lilting tune of a violin joined by a guitar and even a horn.

He threw open the doors, flowing inside with all the force of an arriving cyclone. The lanterns shook on their hooks, a few blowing out, their glass cages shattering as they tossed about. The band on the stage stopped their tune immediately. The prancing fiddler paused, bow ringing out one last note. Getting up from their chairs, the rest of the players took flight, leaving behind their instruments with a clatter and hurrying towards the back door. He only laughed. He would find them.

As he turned his attention back to the stage, back to the woman standing there, fiddle in hand, dressed in black. He noted her studying eyes and the smile on her face. It was odd. She didn't seem to be one of the folk from the village; she didn't seem familiar. Whatever scheme this was, the girl would pay the toll this time.

Behind him came the clap of the two massive doors closing, a bolt sliding into place between them. He turned his gaze, looking through his own shifting form, and spotted a few of the sheriff's men run by the windows. He noticed then just how empty this hall was for a party.

"Joe," called a voice emerging from between the curtains draped behind the stage. Her tone was as flat and dead as autumn leaves yet carried like a judge's command in the hall. When his silver eyes fell upon her, that wicked grin crept upon his lips once more. Here was one who bore the skin of the blue folk, here was one with the eyes of a killer among their kind, and guns strapped to her sides like a cazadora. Before his death he had heard tales of them, of their betrayal and exile.

"It seems that I have gained some fame.
Tell me dear, who speaks my name?"

Joe said, drifting forward, winds carrying him like a hummingbird in flight.

"I am Yamira Garzia, Redhand of Charn, Daughter of Torem's Bane," the Blue Lady said, her wide brimmed hat pulled low over burning eyes. "I offer you a choice: leave this valley and the people be or be banished back to the eternal night."

Laughter escaped his dead lips, and he felt the corners of his mouth crack as his gleaming eyes narrowed on the cazadora. He didn't have a body per se, but he had the remembrance of one, and now that remembrance was howling with amusement.

"You call me here and deliver a threat?
It's been just a moment and we've only
just met!
Many years now this place, my home,
I've made.

These people owe me much, a high debt
not paid."

The Shai woman shook her head and tilted her hat back, looking Joe in the eye. The wind around her tossed her loose hair about, and as the streams of air flowed in from the windows they shook the glass panes and shattered a few. She put her hands on her guns, and said, "You were sent to your first grave unfairly. This second you have dug for yourself."

6

Yami stared at the thing swaying in the wind before her, a decaying man dressed in a tattered tailored suit hanging as though from an invisible noose. His body was translucent as water, his silver eyes peering at her with a tangible hatred. She doubted if a bullet could even harm him. Either her plan worked or it didn't. For a moment she was grateful Isa had gone with her father, still not speaking to him, but now away from the eye of this horror.

Yami took one hand off her pistol and reached for a vial hung from a belt loop. Joe followed her movement, still gauging her, still looking at her like a new toy arrived and was ready to be broken. The vial was filled with a red sand that turned like starlight in the glass. She held it alight in the dwindling lantern glow and said, "Do you know why spirits fear salt?"

Joe tilted his grinning death's head and stared at her sidelong. She could see a rip in his face, a window into the rotting illusion within.

"It purifies what it touches, binds what runs afoul with the living," Yami said. She uncorked the vial and watched for some reaction on the thing's face. "It can even be carried on the wind."

She tossed the vial and the effect was immediate. The red salt was sucked up in the whirlwind around Joe, tossed in his spinning vortex like blood mixing in water. The specter hanging there with a neck turned askew began to scream, thrashing this way and that as he clawed at his own body. Yami had to duck as he moved her way, still flailing in pain but filled with enough clarity of mind to attack her while he could.

She drew one of her guns as she dodged, rolling across the stage while June ducked to the floor, fiddle tumbling out of her hand and a set of two silver coins replacing it. The Blue Lady placed two shots on the specter, which did little to stop him but kept him disoriented. The two cazadoras moved in synchronization, Yami going left while June went right.

One of the first lessons Yami's not-father had taught her was how to make a protection ring, an arrangement of silver pieces that could be used to keep evil out. And in a pinch, it could also be used to keep evil sealed in.

Yami pulled the last two silver pieces from her pocket and flicked the coins towards Joe. Each was pressed with a rune in their centers, the protective eye of the Sightless God. They skidded to a halt behind Joe and to his left. When the specter tried to pass the path of either coin, he howled with curses in an evil tongue. Across from her, June mimicked her motion, sending two silver pieces skidding across the floorboards and paralleling the path of the other coins, forming a square, blocking off any avenue of retreat.

> *"If you think this shall keep me trapped,*
> *it's your neck that will soon be snapped*
>
> *. . ."*

Joe said, his face still twisted in a hateful grin, showing rows of rotted teeth gripped by blackened gums.

"Doesn't need to hold you long," June said, taking her silver dagger from her belt and cutting an inscription on the floor. It was more of the olden script, words of hollowing, shapes of unmaking.

Yami began to speak. The words coming from her mouth seemed to weigh heavy in the air, their power felt even over the howl of the wind still tossing everything in the room this way and that. She knew the incantations well, had studied them at her not-father's tutelage since she was a girl. Their meaning was unknown to most, and even June had difficulty even remembering what the words even were half the time. They had that effect on the world around them, a world that no longer wished to know them and would rather forget.

As the Blue Lady began her incantation, she saw the familiar glow begin to come from the coins around Joe, a harsh light the color of the sun's kiss. Looking too long at that light had driven men to madness before, and it was for this reason that Yami only holstered her gun and stared at the floorboards near her feet. She might send Joe away and lose herself in the process, a fate no living soul would survive.

"You'd deny me what I am owed?!
Destroy my spirit before they reap what
they've sowed?!"

Joe said, his clawed hands running down and tearing through the ghoulish mask that was his face, revealing the white bone beneath. He began to laugh, a loathsome sound that set both women's teeth on edge.

"Death may be nigh,
but not yet for you and not for I . . ."

Suddenly Yami's chant broke, she turned just in time to see a windowpane come loose from its groove and barrel towards her. She only had a moment to raise her arm and keep the glass from cutting into her face. Instead, she felt the sharp bite as the serrated edge dug into her forearm, blood flowing down her skin and soaking her shirt sleeve.

The force of the blow knocked her off her feet and to the ground. June tried to catch her, tried to block the woman's crash with her body, but she wasn't fast enough, she couldn't stop Yami from sliding into the ring of coins and breaking the shape. The light pouring from the metal died, like a candle being snuffed out. And both cazadoras looked up to see the greenish shape in the darkness wave their way as he drifted to the end of the hall, ripping the doors free and escaping into the night.

"Isa and the sheriff!" Yami said, picking herself up off the ground and scooping the coins with her. If they'd had just a few more then they could have made a stronger circle, could have avoided this entirely.

"Can we outrun the wind?" June asked, helping Yami along, eying the wound on her arm with eyes that showed too much white.

"We must try."

Yami moved as fast as she could, leaving June behind easily, despite her wound. She could feel the lightness in her head now, but she couldn't let it get the best of her. There was no way she was letting him have the girl, no way she was letting it end this way.

The door was off the hinges, revealing an open mouth of blackness, screaming echoing in the dark, followed by wicked laughter.

"Stay away from her!" Harlow bellowed, his voice trailing off.

Yami dashed inside, gun holstered for all the good it could do, silver coins in her fist. There was no telling if what she planned would work, but she needed to try. Try or die.

When she reached the Sheriff's office, she found a grisly scene. A body lay on the floor, blood pooling across the floorboards. Yami noted that the figure wasn't dead, his chest rising and falling. Harlow looked up at her, a deep wound on the side of his neck, where something had gnawed at his skin, tearing away a great portion of his flesh. He was still breathing, but his face was pale, and his hands fought desperately to press down on his wound, to stop the bleeding.

Hovering above was the figure of a woman held in spindly arms, over her shoulder a set of silver eyes staring with glee. Isa and Joe looked like they were suspended by wires, two chimes carried on the wind. The look of terror on the girl's face made Yami's blood froth, and she felt the muscles of her chin clench as she took a step inside.

"You're too late my little lass,
Sheriff here's about to pass.
Before he goes,
I think it's fair he knows,
his daughter still pays for what I'm
owed,"

Joe said, a single long nail running along Isa's cheek, leaving a red cut in her skin where her tears flowed.

"Damn you, Joe . . ." Harlow said, his voice coming out like a rasping whisper. "Leave her be . . . this was my mistake . . ."

Isa spoke up, managing to say through Joe's grip, "No . . . Daddy . . ."

There were tears in Harlow's eyes as he said, "I was the one who killed him. Me. The others in town were all talk, never doing what was necessary. They saw him going about, perverting our home, stealing our women. They did nothing. That night William tried to stop me, tried to convince me. But I gave him what he deserved . . ."

Laughter again from Joe, and Yami noted how his grip on the girl's neck tightened, the rise and fall of her chest freezing.

"See now girl, how your daddy thinks?
He kills as easily as he blinks.
To think he swore to protect and serve,
but it's he who'll get what he deserves."

"Close your eyes, Isa!" Yami shouted, dashing then, rushing across the room in two strides, and launching herself over the body of the fallen sheriff. She'd worked the silver coins between each groove of her fingers so the edges faced out. As she moved, she repeated the words her father had taught her, repeated the song of the ancients and felt the warmth in her fist. It was a searing pain, but for the moment she didn't mind. She only had a moment before Joe could react, before he could bring his claws across the hollow of Isa's throat.

She cranked back her fist and dove for Joe. In the final instant before she made contact with the specter's jaw, she noticed two things. One, thankfully the girl had squeezed her eyes shut. If it didn't work, at least Isa wouldn't have to watch her die. Second, Joe's smile was gone, his eyes fixed on her now glowing white knuckles, his grip loosening on Isa as he tried to defend himself. He was too slow, and there was no hate or even anger in him then; only fear.

The flash of light was blinding, and Yami had to squeeze her eyes shut at the last possible second before she tore through the creature. Even with them closed the light was so bright it was disorienting. Like seeing the sun appear out of the dead of night. The feeling as her fist ripped into Joe was like plunging her hand into ice water, followed by a sharp burn as though she'd taken hold of hot coals. There came a scream that stretched into the howl of the wind, growing louder and louder until it nearly deafened her. She didn't know if it was Joe, or her own voice as she felt her skin begin to crackle and blister. Then, ears still ringing, the noise dimmed to an echo carried away through the broken windows and out into the night air. When the last of the winds faded and Yami heard the soft thud of Isa resting back on solid ground, she opened her eyes. Her hand wasn't going to be drawing a gun anytime soon, and the smoke trailing off of it had a distinctly porkish smell, but she held it close to herself as she turned to check on the girl.

Isa was on her knees beside her father. He was lying still, only the faintest trace of life in his eyes. He tried to open his mouth to say something, anything to her, but his mouth froze forever. Isa pushed her face into his chest without much care of his blood getting on her. Yami stood over the girl a long while before June arrived. As she waited, there were only sobs on the wind.

7

A few days after the dust had settled, people began to walk about in the streets of the town again, no longer resembling mice fearing a cat. Yami set off from the memorial erected around the ruins of the sheriff's station. Flowers from every garden in town had been piled on the steps, and there was already talk of rebuilding what was lost. With the bounty promised to her in a drawstring bag at her hip, Yami wished them well but knew she'd never see their labor's fruits.

By the time she met up with the others the sun was high overhead. They had agreed to meet by the memento tree on their way out of town, once June had gotten the horses and the bags were packed. Yami spied Isa tying something to the lowest branch of the tree, something that looked all too familiar as Yami approached.

"Ready to go?" she asked, wincing as a twinge of pain flared up her bandaged and splinted arm. The burns had begun healing from the explosion, but it would be a while before the bones knit back together. The doctor who'd set her warned the ache might never fade.

June was leaning against the tree, trinkets swaying around her head. "Miss Harlow here wanted to leave something behind before we went. Couldn't say no," she said, wheezing a little on the last word.

Yami caught Isa's eye, and the girl smiled. That distant look on her face was far from gone, but it had receded for the time being. "My father wasn't a good man, but even he deserves to be remembered," she said, walking past Yami and towards the horses. She had taken her father's steed from the stable by the office, and taunted that she was a practiced rider. "Y'all better keep up."

The cazadoras followed the girl, however Yami spared one last look at the tree, one last glance at the final memento tied there. It was a half-melted coin with an eye pressed into the face, one of the few from the other night. She smiled and thought, *sometimes the only way to escape a debt is to outlive it.*

About the Authors

Ross Carmona

Ross Carmona is an Orlando, Florida based writer of dark fantasy, speculative fiction, and everything in between. When he isn't grinding away at the nine-to-five, he's crafting forgotten worlds and weaving the lives of those who wander there. This story is his first published work—and the first of many to successfully escape into reality.

Oscar Chavira, Jr.

Oscar Chavira Jr. is a licensed mental health therapist from Hereford, a rural town in the Texas panhandle. He is a current member of the Caprock Writers and Illustrators Association, and he has his blog where he currently documents his writing journey. Oscar's main genres are horror and thriller, putting protagonists in situations where they get to explore the themes of dread and stagnation in the situations they find themselves in.

George Cottonwood

George Cottonwood is a storyteller with a passion for grit, action, and the untamed frontier, specializing in hardboiled westerns and men's adventure fiction. An avid outdoorsman, he enjoys hunting, camping, and fishing with his wife and young son. In his day job, he works as a communications specialist for a faith-based child foster care agency in South Texas. He has written for Stand Firm Magazine, Texas Parks and Wildlife Magazine, Saddlebag Dispatches, and

Veritas Entertainment. You can find his fiction work at georgecottonwoodbooks.wordpress.com.

Tony Garcia

Tony Garcia lives in the Arizona mountains creating and running games, sketching, and writing. He has several published stories in multiple anthologies and other works, but the biggest project is his original roleplaying game – "Dystopian Dawn". The core set (Player's Guide and Game Master's Guide) launched in 2023, since then Tony wrote and published several adventure and world books. He is set to publish the 13th book by the end of 2025, with sights on new worlds for 2026 and beyond. A prolific indie supporter, Tony collaborates with many authors and creators, and only hires indie Artists for his projects.

His story "Trajak Tale of the Last Ranger" is based on characters who originally appeared in the Dystopian Dawn source adventure books "Cowboys & Mutants!" and "Vikings & Robots!".

In 2025 you can find him running games online via Discord, chatting with creatives on X, and in-person at multiple upcoming conventions in Tucson. For more information about Dystopian Dawn, you can check out his website www.fract uredbrainstudios.com .

Curtis Moore

Curtis Moore lives, works, and writes in rural Nevada. He has written articles on scientific conflict, and presented on levels of conflict in fiction at the League of Utah Writers' Pre-Quill conference in April 2023. The Silverstage Players selected his play *Behavioral Science* for their Writer's Spotlight in July, 2023. His nonfiction essay *Co-parenting With Cormac McCarthy* was shortlisted in The Milk House's Best of Rural Writing 2023 Contest. His published short stories include *The Quincey Morris Society*, and *The Breaker in the Sky*, and *Outlaw Magic*. A full list of Curtis' published works can be found on his website at curtismoo rewrites.com.

Michael John Petty

Michael John Petty is an author, podcaster, and filmmaker with a deep love of storytelling. When he isn't writing, he enjoys scenic drives, mountainous hikes, fellowship with his local church, and a good Western. Michael is the creator of The Bear-tooth Mountain Archive, which began with *The Beast of Bear-tooth Mountain*. His short story, *The Devil's Left Hand*, won the Spur Award for Best Western Short Fiction in 2025. He currently resides in North Idaho with his wonderful wife and beautiful daughters. You can find Michael intermittently on his Substack, *Further Up & Further In*, which doubles as his newsletter.

Benjamin Winters

Benjamin Winters is a cowboy turned techie with a love for storytelling and tall tales. Taking his experiences as a fourth generation rancher, and looking to the future with his work in technology, Benjamin loves to explore the conflict of tradition and innovation in his writing. He lives with his wife and two cats in Virginia, where he is roundin' up letters instead of dogies. You can connect with him on Instagram by following @benjaminwinterswrites for new stories.